ANANSI'S WEB

Derek Mola

Cover Art: Luisa Galstyan. ISBN: 978-8-218-28559-3
Printed in the United States of America 2024

This book is for my MOTHER, FATHER, BROTHER for always supporting me. And for my TACOY, PEPPERE, NONNA, and PAPPA, with love.

Contents

ANANSI'S WEB

Prologue

Once in the world, there were no stories, as they were all held by the god Nyame. One day, Anansi went to Nyame and asked him if he could have the stories. Anansi was but a simple spider, and known to be a trickster amongst the other animals. Entertaining his request, Nyame gave Anansi four labors: Onini the python, the hornet Mmoboro, the leopard Osebo, and the fairy Mmoatia. Taking on the challenge, Anansi captured all the creatures and presented them to Nyame. Admitting defeat and impressed with Anansi, the god handed over the stories to Anansi and declared him the new god of stories. And Anansi shared them with the world, spreading knowledge and joy.

Deep in the forests of Ghana, if you know where to look, you can find the hut of Anansi. You can find his hut hanging from a spider's web, and if you tell him a joke, he might shrink you down and invite you in.

"Why is a dog like a tree? Because they both lose their bark once they're dead."

Young Kweku did this to find Anansi's hut when he made the week-long trek across the forests. When he was inside the hut, he noticed that it was much more prominent on the inside than on the outside. And there wasn't much to look at except a throne at the end of the room.

Kweku walked towards the throne, hoping to sit upon it. For he was exhausted, and it looked oh so comfortable.

"Trying to make ourselves at home, I see?" said a voice.

Kweku turned around, and there he was the great Anansi. He stood 10 feet tall, the top half of a man and the bottom half of a spider: muscular, black skin, long black hair, and a burly beard. Kweku bowed before him.

"I apologize for my rudeness. I am weary from my travels." explained Kweku.

"You dare to disturb me! Tell me your business quickly so you might be on your way!" he replied.

"Great Anansi, god of all stories, I have traveled many miles to come and visit you. To ask you if you would grant me one wish?" said Kweku.

"You are but a lad of 12. You are not even a man. I should cook you up and eat you for my dinner for having come to me with such a foolish idea. Most men do not get this close to my hut unless I allow it. But…your joke did very much make me laugh. Very well, what is your wish?" asked Anansi.

"Please, would you tell me one of your extraordinary spider stories?" asked Kweku.

The god laughed in Kweku's face. "Your wish amuses me! Why do you want me to tell you a story?" asked Anansi.

"I am quite bored. All day long in my village of the Akan people, I listen to my parents, elders, and friends; every day, it is the same old thing. It is driving me mad! So I have come to you with the simple request of telling me a story that will cure my boredom." explained Kweku.

Anansi was silent and thought about the young boy's request for quite some time. He paced around the room, his spider legs tapping along the ground.

"Alright young man, you made the journey all the way, you have shown me respect, and most importantly, you have made me laugh. I will tell you a story. Better yet, I will tell you many a tale! Come, and look above!" shouted Anansi.

As Kweku looked above, the room became illuminated by the sudden appearance of thousands of fireflies. An orange glow lit up the room, and Kweku noticed, on the ceiling was a giant spider web. The web glistened, and each strand was flowing with energy.

"This is the source of all stories, my boy. The source of all life, some may say. For what are we, if not a collection of stories? Each strand of this web is a different story. A story of love, a story of tragedy, a story of life, or a story of death. Sit on my throne, choose a strand, and begin the tale." explained Anansi.

Kweku sat on the throne, which was as comfy as he had imagined. He then looked up at the massive spider web.

"How about that one?" pointed Kweku. "Good choice." said Anansi.

Tear Drops

The Loch is calm on this cold summer morning. A wave did not crash, nor did a fish swim. The salty air could sting the nostrils, but the beauty of the Loch could bring tears to the eyes. The waves haphazardly threw shells and seaweed during the night, the morning sun casting its image across the water, its orange glow contrasting with the loch's darkest blue. Across the water, mountains stretch as far as the eye can see. To get to the Loch, you have to cross the forest. Thick oak and spiky pines await you, along with its fair share of woodland creatures. And if you go far enough, there lay a village, and in this village is the source of my sustenance. Here comes one now. A poor, drunken man walking along the shore. Bobbing and weaving around the seashells, careful not to have his boots touch the water. The man, probably still drunk from the night before, is taking a lovely morning stroll. I am waiting a few feet away for him to stumble upon me. Not many people are willing to approach a wild stallion anymore. Especially one seen wandering around the forest at night. Nowadays, horses are already in captivity and are forced to breed against their will, and the babies are trained from day one. So I've had to change from my proper form to something that will easily manipulate the human mind. Women are not so privy to these desires, but men are driven by them. Lust is the essence of man, unable to control it and unable to disobey its beckoning call. The poor, drunken man stumbles upon me. I have taken the form of a young woman, naked and dead. I've taken the appearance as though I have drowned.

At first, he is shocked. Looking around the beach, he tries to find someone to help. But he is alone. Just him and I. He looks me over, at first embarrassed by my exposed privates. I can see his cheeks becoming red. He kneels before me, putting his hand over my neck, feeling for a pulse, touching my skin. But as he feels my neck, his hand slowly creeps toward my breasts—a slight smirk on his face. You can see the excitement in his eyes. And this is precisely the moment when I strike. Kelpies have a remarkable ability. A gland in the brain's right hemisphere allows us to sweat an adhesive through our pores, sticking the skin of our prey to our body. It's a beautiful skill, able to entrap our prey in a moment's touch. As his hand goes down my spine, it sticks to my back, unable to move. He tries to pry them off, but it is too late. Then, my transformation. The first thing that begins to appear is my tail, which surprised him quite a bit. A long, black tail grows between my haunches, my hands and feet become hooves, my arms and legs elongated, my body wide, and I grow more extensive. My skin is becoming leathery, and black fur grows all over me. My neck stretches out, and my mane grows long, proud, and soaking wet. The man, his hand still stuck, now clings to me like a child to his mother. Holding onto my back for dear life, holding onto the woman who had just turned into a horse before his eyes.

"A Kelpie! I meant ye' no harm! Let me go. I'll tell none ye' live in these waters!" said the drunkard.

With a neigh that echoes in the morning sky, I run towards the water for a few feet. Then with all the grace I could muster, I leap into the depths below, dragging my assailant down with me. I won't speak for others of my kind, but the adrenaline and the fear make the meat richer. I turn my head around to watch him. His eyes almost bulging out of his head, he tries to bring his hands to his neck, but they're still stuck to me. As he gasps for air, the bubbles rise to the surface, filled with hopeless cries that never reach ears. By the time I get to the floor of the Loch, the man is dead.

***

It's been months since that day. One man can only satisfy the stomach for so long. And dead fish floating along the current is not the best tasting. I must find another. Upon the shore, I prepare myself for another entrapment. But changing into my human form is quite unpleasant. My body is so small and restrictive, and I have never really accustomed myself to walking upright. Nevertheless, I am here again, preparing to lie on the shore and make my body cold, pale, and beautiful.

"Miss, are you alright?!" said a voice.

I rose to my feet. A man, sitting on the sandhill, is watching me prepare myself. I turn around and run towards the water. But before I can, I feel a hand grab my shoulder. Concerned, he chases after me.

"Miss! Where are you going? We should get you some clothes." shouted the man.

His hand, upon my shoulder. This the perfect moment. The fool has no idea. I can stick his skin to mine and drag him right into the Loch: easy prey and an easy meal. I look into his eyes. I want to see the fear in them. But… they are beautiful. A deep blue, more profound than the Loch itself. His face is soft and sharp. And his curly brown hair sways in the wind. I couldn't. I couldn't bring myself to do it. I brush his hand off, back away, and quickly dive into the depths below.

***

After that incident with the man, I hid. Indeed, he would've warned the townsfolk of the legendary Kelpie spotted at the Loch. But nobody bothered the waters in those weeks. I assume they didn't believe him. Since I have been stuck underwater for a long time, I decided to prance around in my proper form. At night, the beach is filled with late-night lovers and drunken vandals. I sneak from the water, disguised as one of them, and then transform into a beautiful, black mare. The darkness of the trees should keep me concealed, at least until the beach clears. I walk through the forest to the edge of the village. I peer over the bushes and twigs at the midnight people. They are singing and dancing, laughing at each other, the men holding their women tight, their fires ever raging. Warmth. That's something that I've never known, something I've longed for. The warmth of a fire, the warmth of clothing, the warmth of the sun, the warmth of another's flesh. The sea is dark, cold, and unforgiving. If the sea ever had a heart, I believe a whale ate it, and when it shat it out, it sank to the bottom, slowly being eaten by bottom feeders. The souls of dead sailors wander the seas, wondering why they should never see the kingdom of heaven. The sea is heartless, and I do not think I shall know anything else.

As I wonder and watch, I see him—the man who tried to speak to me and knows of my true identity. Again, I stare into his eyes. This is dangerous. Kelpies do not receive or give affection. We are the sea's denizens, preying on men's affection for the female form. But from time to time, we, too, fall prey to man's charms. Many Kelpies I have known have become a man's property if he knows how. If a man can throw a saddle on our backs, we are theirs to ride for eternity. I will lose my magic, my ability to transform, my ability to live underwater. I will become an average horse for the rest of my days. I do not know this man's intentions, but they can only lead to my demise. I turn around and make my leave back to the sea.

***

I can see him waiting for me above the water. It's been several weeks since our chance encounter, and he sits on the sand daily, staring out into the water. Sometimes an hour, sometimes a few minutes, but continually every day. I do not understand it. I am the Kelpie of legend and the story mothers tell their children at night so they stay away from the water. I am the creature sailors fear; I do not understand why this man waits for me. Well, perhaps I will give him what he wants. Maybe he wishes to die, or perhaps he is just an imbecile. No matter, food is all the same. Slowly, in my naked female form, I appear from the Loch. I stand still and wait to see what he plans to do. Maybe the fool truly is in love with me, a mistake on his part. He sits there, staring at me.

"You better cover yourself up, or they'll for sure be on to you, Miss." he says.

He throws me a towel. He doesn't change his position, and he doesn't even seem impressed with my appearance. It lands on me, but I throw it to the ground. I am dumbfounded.

"I am Kelpie of legend, sir. You had best fear me or perish." I threaten. Still, nothing. He stayed seated.

"I think if that were true, then I would've been dead the first time I met you." he says.

His coy nature was getting on my nerves. I have very little patience for the sarcasm of
men.

"You don't seem to be afraid. Well, you should be. I have killed hundreds of men, and I will gladly add you t-"

"Would you like some cheese?" he interrupts.

I had not even noticed that he was sitting on a blanket, a basket beside him. He opened the basket and pulled out a block of cheese, a roll of bread, and a bottle of wine.

"I do not know if you have ever had any of this before, but I was wondering if you cared to join me?" he asks.

I am speechless. How dare he. I should storm off, but my chest is beginning to fluster, my heart is beating, and I can't think straight. What is happening to me? I start inching my way toward him.

"And if I should refuse? What if I was to grab you right now and bring you into the sea with me? Dragging you down to the ocean floor until your breath is gone and you become my meal for the next month?" I threaten.

Surely, this should scare him. At this point, I have no interest in eating the man. My appetite is gone, and I have made myself vulnerable. No, this was now an exercise in my reputation. To show my dominance and to keep the fear in the hearts of men alive.

"Suit yourself." he said.

He begins packing the items back into the basket, the cheese, the bread, the wine, and even the blanket, about to leave me behind. To turn his back on me. Me?! In a rage, I grab his arm. The secretion of the liquid begins to leak through the pours in my hand, latching onto his skin. He turns around, and I see the fear in his eyes for the first time. Finally, he thinks he can tame this creature. Woo me into some fantasy where he conquers what can not be conquered. But he is surely mistaken. I will drag him into the sea, where he will keep my belly warm. My teeth grit, my grip strong, and my eyes filled with fire. Yet, he remains calm. How can he be so calm? I look into his eyes and see that same compassion from before.

"I don't mean any harm to you. I just figured you could use a friend." he says.

A friend. A Kelpie does not have friends. She has the sea and the bottom feeders. That is the life of a kelpie. I loosen my grip. He seems hesitant, but he begins to lay out the blanket and spreads the food again. I take the towel he throws and wrap it around my body. I sit beside him, and we eat his food.

"So Miss Kelpie, the sea scourge, what is it like? Down there in the Loch?" he asks.

I have never been asked this before. There are few creatures to talk to, and the eels and carp do not converse well.

"It is dark, it is cold, and it is lonely. Perfect for a creature like me." I answer. His eyes grew sad and concerned.

"A creature like you deserves warmth, happiness, a bed, servants at your side, and a palace to rule!" he says mockingly.

I stare at him angrily. Jokes are something I do not take likely.

"Such kind words, but what is your game? Why all this? You do not mean to bring my corpse back to town, do you? The triumphant hero that slayed the Kelpie?" I ask mockingly.

"No, no, nothing like that. To be quite truthful, I am an outcast myself. I spend my days painting, working very little, drinking, and painting some more. I am seen as a dullard in the community. But painting is what I love doing." he answers.

"But that still avoids my question." I say.

"I knew you were a kelpie the first time I saw you." he says. I am shocked. Men do not see through the ruse so easily.

"Kiley, the old drunkard, was last seen roaming towards the loch the other night. Nobody has found the body, and they say he probably drowned in the sea. But normally, his body would have washed up after a few weeks. So, I had my suspicions that there may have been a kelpie near the waters. And sure enough, here you are. Plus, there are not many wild horses in these parts. And strange horse prints in the sand? Not the best look." he said.

This one is brilliant, too smart for his own good.

"It's alright. I won't say anything. The old codger was a waste anyway, drinking his life away. But he did have a brother, a family, and people who cared for him. You have the entire ocean for feasting. Why do you kill us?" he said, sadness in his voice.

"I watch you. You men. You take what you want and do not consider the consequences.

And I do not regret taking lives that do not respect others." I say, anger in my eyes.

"You think of us as monsters, but what of you? You, the nightmares of children, the scourge of the sea, the fear in the hearts of men. Are you truly better than us?" he asks.

"You are the strangest man I have ever met." I tell him.

"Well, you are not the first women to say that to me." he replies. That makes us laugh, something I do not often do. "Michael…my name is Michael." he says.

"I do not have a name." I say.

"Well, then we shall have to give you one? How about?... Kel! Short for Kelpie." he says. "I like it." I say.

"So, what will you do now, Kel?" he says. A wave of panic washes over me.

"I've been out too long, and it's a wonder that no one has seen me. I must leave." I say hurriedly.

I get up, remove the blanket, and run back toward the ocean.

"Wait!" he shouts. "Can I see you tomorrow? I'll meet you back here in the afternoon."

Does he want to see me again? Even though I am a monster? I say nothing. I turn around back towards the ocean and run. With one great leap, I dive in, swimming to the bottom.

***

I have come to the surface early. The sun hides behind the clouds, and the world has turned grey. As I transform into my female form, I become aware for the first time that I am completely nude. Something I would never give a second thought, but my cheeks begin to flush thinking about Michael arriving and having nothing to cover up with. But knowing him, I am sure he will bring me another blanket. Maybe he'll even get me some clothes? Could he mean to take me to the village? I can see it. I am a new girl, freshly arriving in the village. Maybe he met me while taking a walk? Maybe I have escaped some terrible marriage? Perhaps I am a nomad, traveling here and there. A girl who has never had a place is looking for somewhere to belong. He will introduce me to his friends and take me to the tavern for a drink. The others will gawk and whisper their gossip.

"This new girl will only bring trouble" they'll say.

But I won't care. Michael won't care. We will sit there till the sun goes down, drinking, eating, and telling stories of our exploits. And when the night is over, I can go home with him?...

During all this pondering, I have not paid mind to my surroundings. I look around at the Loch before me. The cold wind blows, loud in force. Leaves fall in numbers as the trees sway. The waves crash, rivaling the thunder in the sky. The sea worms wriggle the water pockets in the sand bubble. I can even hear the buzzards swarming the dead seagull a few feet away. And yet, all seems quiet. Quiet, like before lightning strikes, before a lover's kiss, like...before a predator strikes its prey. As quickly as the thought arrived, the gang of men also jumped from their positions behind the trees. Four came at me with spears and swords; one even threw a net over me. They slice at me, prod me, weakening my defenses. Their hands never touch me."Oy, don't kill her, lads." says the leader.

As he walks over to me, the others are holding me down. I'm losing a lot of blood, I'm nauseous, my vision is blurry, my focus is faltered, and my head is ringing.

"That was pretty stupid of ye' to lounge around in the open. Yer waitin' fer someone?" he
asks.

I manage to spit some of my blood at him. He smacks me across the face.

"Lousy bitch! You killed my brother Kiley! Kiley was too afraid of da water. No way he'd go swimming, even if drunker than a skunk. I kept coming to the beach late at night, and that's when I noticed the strange hoof prints. That's when I thought…damn Kelpies! I know ye probably think me a dullard, but I know a thing or two of the kelpies. Flip her over, boys, and hold her down." he demands.

I struggle as best, but four against one is not a fair fight. The leader unlatches something from around his chest. I noticed it before, a brown leather strap. I assume it to be a satchel of some kind. But watching him unlatch it, horror grows inside me for the first time. It is a saddle meant for the riding of wild horses. I am to become his property.

"Help me! Please! Someone help!" I scream.

The shame poisons my blood. The screams echo into the Loch and the forest, but the bottom feeders and ants are the only creatures to hear them. They hold down my arms and legs. My skin secretes the liquid, sticking their skin to mine, but they are too strong for me. Their leader puts his foot down onto my back, leans to me, and whispers into my ear, "It's a damn shame. Ye sure is a beauty". Then he places the saddle onto my back, strapping the belt around my waist.

"Let her go, lads!" he shouts.

To my amazement, they can release their hands from my arms. The secretion has stopped. My body begins to feel weak, and I start to shake violently. I have no control. Slowly but surely, I transform back into my proper form. My horse form. I am stuck here, a beast of nature, forced to ride this man till my days are done. They circle me, laughing at me.

"Get her up, lads!" the leader says.

They force me up from the sand. I whinney and neigh as loud as possible, but no good it does. I am a filthy mare now.

"Ye still is a beauty, even without the breasts. But you've still got a crackin' arse!" the leader jokes.

This makes them howl with laughter. I kick at them, trying to make a run for the village, and find Michael. Maybe, somehow, he'd be able to recognize me. But one of those brutes pulls out a whip. And before I can get far, a sharp sting goes against my legs. I go down hard.

Crashing into the sand. They run over and pick me back up. I can barely stand.

"Let this be a lesson. Ye ain't ever leavin' me. Yer mine now, darling. Till I'm dead in the ground." he says.

Mounted upon my back, we ride into town. I feel disgusting. The saddle rubbed against my skin, the weight of this man crushing my soul slowly. I am defeated.

In town, we stop at a local pub. There are 4 horses tied down in front, waiting for their masters to arrive. The other men climb up on their steeds, patting them like you would a docile pet. I cannot even look at them. As they mount, a familiar face exits the bar. Michael.

"Oh, hello there, Sean. Nice day out." Michael says kindly. "Aye, tis indeed." replies Sean, the leader.

His eyes are so sweet, and I can see something red and yellow on his hands. He must have just finished painting.

"That's a nice steed you have there." says Michael. "Just purchased her the other day." says Sean, lying.

"Well, she is a beauty. I'm sure I'll see you gentlemen around," says Michael.

"Uh, not quite. See, the lads and I will be heading off from this point. I was living with me brother, and with him missing, I'd say it's about time we moved on from here." says Sean.

Leaving town?! No! It can't be! I begin to whinny, and I cannot be going! Not now! "Woah there!" yells Sean.

"Seems to be rowdy this one." says Michael.

"Oh, don't ye worry? She'll learn to behave herself. Won't ye darling?" says Sean, patting my head.

I can feel the firmness in his hand, the anger in his voice. I would pay for that on the road, indeed.

"Well, I guess this is goodbye then, Sean. And goodbye to you, beautiful." says Michael, looking towards me.

With a gentle hand, he wipes the tears from my eyes.

"Now, if you'll excuse me, gentlemen, I have an appointment." Michael says, walking towards the Loch with a slight smile.

"Alright, lads, let's head out!" yells Sean.

I turn my head, watching him walk away to the Loch. I want to run towards him, and I want to scream and kick, anything to make him understand. But with a jab from Sean's heel, I am forced to trot down the trail in the opposite direction.

"Next town is a three-day ride. Be prepared, lads."

After three days of riding, we went to a new town with new faces.

Alone, I may be, but there is one thing about Kelpies that Sean does not know. It is scarce for a Kelpie to shed tears. Our tears have magical properties, and whoever wipes away the tears of a Kelpie will be bonded to the Kelpie till the end of time. Michael, by this time, you will think I have betrayed you. You will think of me for what I have told you. That I am a heartless monster of the sea. Though you may think this, unbeknownst to you, our hearts are now in twine. The feeling will always be there. You may find someone new, someone, who will fill your soul with such joy, someone to laugh with you, someone to hold onto, someone to keep warm in the night. But regardless, you will not be able to help but feel empty. Somewhere, deep down inside of you, an endless cavern, a dark hole that can never be filled. And no matter how hard you try, empty it will remain.

Dragon's Gate

Walking along the mountainside path, Shun Long watches the waterfall crash into the pool of water below. He has been on this journey for three nights, trekking up the mountain along the Bayan Har trail. 14,000 feet up, the world seems small and insignificant. At this height, the clouds above the mountain tops look like foam above water, the peaks breaking through to the heavens. To the left of him, the roaring rapids crash through rock and stone. Sloshing and splashing, foam rises above the surface. In the river, gently and gracefully traveling along with the current, a single carp. A beautiful orange and white, the light shines off its scales, making it look like a creature of divine nature. As he observes, a roar shakes the Earth above. Louder than the thundering of a storm, an angel floating down from the tallest mountain peak. Larger than comprehension, the body of a snake, scales of a carp, head of a camel, horns of a giant stag, paws like a tiger, and claws like an eagle. Falling through the clouds, Shun Long thought it dead. But it was already taking off into the heavens as fast as it appeared. Serpentine motions in the sky; its tail whips a mountain, causing it to crumble and make rocks slide down to the Earth below.

Maybe this was a sign to turn back, or perhaps it was a sign of the greatness awaiting the end of his journey. The Gods work in mysterious ways, and the dragons are mysterious indeed. They play in the mountain tops, secluding themselves from the world of man. Only through meditation are humans allowed to meet the dragons. When one becomes enlightened, a dragon will come down and fly you to heaven. That is the way it has always been. Dragons and humans have always had a distant relationship with each other. But Shun Long will make the journey—the journey to Dragons Gate.

Nobody knows when Dragon's Gate appeared or even how or why. But for centuries, the carp that live in the Yellow River have tried to climb the running rapids. They try to rise to the tallest mountain and reach the Dragon's Gate. It's a long and treacherous journey. The carp must swim upstream, climb through rocks more significant than itself, and fight the strong current. But if a Carp should reach the top and jump off the waterfall, it will turn into a dragon and fly off into the heavens above. No human has ever been to Dragons Gate, and it is forbidden. The dragons do not take kindly to the unenlightened folk. High above heaven, the dragons and the Gods watch humanity, guarding them against disaster and guiding them to join their ranks.

***

His legs begin to give out. He is ready to collapse after seven long travel days, harsh winds, and thin air. But he has arrived. He is greeted by a red archway made of wood. Since the dawn of time Dragons Gate has stood and the paint seems like it was painted this morning.

Fresh, red as an autumn apple. Carved in gold lettering at the top of the arch, it reads: "Here be dragons." The words chilled him to the bone. Ahead of the gate is a thick shroud of fog for which one can see nothing. Frozen in place, he stands grounded like a tree, but like one with dead bark and falling leaves. He is afraid. This was a mistake. The dragon would surely kill him on site.

"Just turn around and head back down the mountain." he thought. "You may enter." said a booming voice.

Coming from inside the gate, the voice awakens him. Now filled with some semblance of courage, he walks into Dragons gate with a deep breath and adjusts his posture. Entering into the fog, every synapse fires, every nerve tingles, and the adrenaline causes his bones to feel like they are on fire. At first, there was nothing. Nothing to see, everything to fear. But then, an intense light blinded him. And soon enough, when he regained sight, he found himself in a lush garden filled with every kind of flower imaginable. A rainbow of Roses, Bluebells, Sunflowers, Angels, Trumpets, and Lavender. It was almost overwhelming. The fog is cleared, the sky became cloudless, and the sun is in full view.

"Come, child. Come closer" said the voice.

That voice seems to be coming from everywhere at once. It frightens him. He walks down the sunflower-laden path till he comes upon it. A large pool, clear and as reflective as a household mirror. It is the forbidden pool where all dragons begin. After the carp climbs and reaches the top, it takes a relaxing dip in the forbidden pool. There it is healed, rejuvenated, and finally transformed into a dragon. After that, all that is left is for the carp to jump off the waterfall. From there, it will take flight, soaring into the heavens.

Shun Long steps into the pool. No one is around, and he is nearly dead from exhaustion. He bathes himself, washing his wounds. He drinks the water, hydrating himself. It seeps into his pores, revitalizing his bones and clearing his pains. He sits there, absorbing the water, absorbing the life force that fuels the Earth. As he does so, the fog reappears, encroaching upon him and covering the field of flowers, the pool, and himself. Nothing can be seen in front of him. Except for a giant shadowy mass floating towards him. It slithers through the fog, writhing like a snake. Its long whiskers push through the air, and its horns enlarge as it gets closer until its eyes meet upon Shun Long. Its snout almost touched him, and its scales looked like it could cut steel. The dragon, floating as graceful as a blade of grass in the summer winds, glides over to Shun Long's decimated body and speaks.

"You do not belong here, human." said the voice.

Shun Long, scrunched down in terror, musters his strength, and stands tall, his back straight and his head high. He looks at the dragon.

"Dragon, angel above, I come here to ask you a simple request. Please…allow me to bathe in this pool, jump from the waterfall, and turn into a dragon." Shun Long pleads.

"You are a monk. I can tell by your garb. You know as well as I that humans may only join the dragons when enlightened or through judgment by the end of life. This is what we have deemed, and so it shall be." described the dragon.

"But, great dragon, I have meditated all my life. I am ready. I know it in my heart. I have served under those all my life, waiting for the time when I would rise above them. And I heard you! I heard you in my dreams! I felt you in my heart! Now is the time. I have risen above them, spiritually and physically. I am higher than all could be! I am with you and the other angels! I am you!" he screams to the dragon.

The dragon brings his head down to Shun Long's level so they are eye to eye.

"If that is how you truly feel, then you will never make it into heaven, and you will never become a dragon. I am sorry." declared the dragon.

A tear sheds from Shun Long's eye and drips down to his cheek. He drops down in defeat, sinking deep into the pool, exhausted. He looks down into the water, looking into his reflection. His face is unrecognizable.

"So what is to become of me now?" he asked.

"I will do you no harm. Make the choice now, bow before the angel, and dedicate yourself to inner peace. The choice is yours." said the dragon.

Shun Long steps out of the pool towards the dragon. He stumbles, almost seeming like he is going to bow. But he continues, walking past the dragon and walking towards the waterfall.

"Oh dragon, you are the great carp that defeated the mountain; alas, I have done the same. I have climbed the mountain, and I have swum in the pool. I have done what no other has done before. I have put faith in you all my life, but it is time I put faith into something else.

Myself. When I jump off the waterfall, through the sheer willpower of the human spirit, I will become a dragon. Think of it. The first human to become a dragon. I will be amongst you." he said.

Shun Long reaches the edge of the waterfall. He looks down. The mist from the roaring falls covers all to be seen, even the bottom. He turns to the dragon. He waits for some lasting wisdom, some words of solace, something that will make him step back from the edge.

But there was nothing. The dragon, already beginning to fly away, looks back to Shun Long, disappointment on his face.

The dragon watches as the man crashes into the rocks below. His scales never formed, his whiskers never grew, and his talons never sprouted. The body travels down the stream, through the rocky mountains, past the floating carp, and into the stream near the local mountain village. The dragon continued to watch the body for the next few days. He watched it decay and rot, the water slowly filling his lungs, small families of fish taking bites of his flesh, and until finally, it was nothing more than a pile of bones resting at the bottom of the river. Never before had the dragon taken an interest in the lives of humans. He felt he was beyond that. But this deeply hurt him. The dragon felt sorry for Shun Long, the lonely monk. The dragon cried a thousand tears, causing a massive storm to sweep across the land and destroy all in its path.

Letters From a Skeleton

*M*y brother was not a bad man, just a confused one. He sent me these letters in the Autumn that he was condemned for murder and sentenced to hang. That was 50 years ago. I was 20 years old and living with my family in the Americas. Efi wanted to stay in México, "too much pride," my mother would always say. I never knew what to make of these letters, and I never knew whether to believe them or not. If I did not think it, my brother went insane in his final days. The guilt of his crimes succumbed to him and drove him mad. But...if I chose to believe these letters, then the world is not what we believe it to be. The world is much stranger and much darker than we have known. After the final letter, I spent every day in fear, looking over my shoulder. Even now, upon my deathbed, staring into the eyes of my children and grandchildren, I am afraid that I

will see the face of evil in my final hours. The same one
that took my brother away.

October 29, 1848
México City, México

Dear Dona,

It was on a rainy night like this when I killed my
Elisa. I had just discovered that she had been unfaithful
to me with a man named Andres. I provided for her, took
care of her, and gave her my love, and this is how I am
repaid? I took my iron, and I went to the tavern, asking if
anyone had seen Elisa or if they knew where the man
Andres lived. The barkeep spoke of how he had seen Elisa
and an unknown man walk toward the edge of town. I
followed the path to a house. I kicked down the door to
find my woman and her lover embracing each other's
arms. I aimed at Andres, but Elisa stepped before him,
taking the bullet. Her body fell to the ground, blood
pouring from her wound. Then I unloaded four more
rounds into Andres. I tried to escape but was soon
surrounded by four officers. There was a time when a

man took care of his business. Now it is all about democracy. Perhaps you and the family were right to move to America. I could not bear to leave our home and live amongst those that wish to destroy it. They have moved me to México City, where I will be hanged in four days. Día de Los Muertos of all days. I am not offered much here, but I am thankful they allowed me to write letters to loved ones before my death. Most inmates might try to escape, kill a guard, or kill themselves. But, I wish to die like a man. I love you, Dona, and I am sorry for any pain I have caused you and the family.

Sincerely,
Efi Esqueleto

October 30, 1848
México City, México

Dear Dona,

I was not planning on writing you another letter, I did not want to burden you anymore, but the most extraordinary thing has happened to me. I write this letter knowing that I am on death's doorstep. You may think that I must have been experiencing guilt and remorse. Maybe you'll believe that God served his judgment early, or perhaps you'll think I went insane from a broken heart. Whatever you feel about me, Dona, I must plead with you to believe me. I have spoken with the other side! God has given me a chance at forgiveness, which has come in the form of a Calaca. Yes, the skeleton doll from Día de Los Muertos has given me a way out of prison and to start life anew. It all started last night after I finished writing the first letter I sent you. I handed it to the guard so they could mail it, and then I fell asleep on my bed. It was still raining, but the moon was shining bright in the sky. It shined into my cell through the back window lined with metal bars. The ground was illuminated, and as I lay on my cot, I began to hear the faintest of whispers.

"Hola, senor. Let me out." the voice said.

Let me out. Over and over again. Let me out, let me out. I stood up and walked over to my cell door. Looking out between the bars, I tried to find the source of the voice, thinking it was one of the other prisoners or a guard playing a trick on us. But no, the voice seemed to be coming from inside my cell. I put my ear to the walls but heard nothing. I looked out at the back window but could see no living soul.

"Let me out, let me out."

Finally, I put my ear to the ground, and the voice became louder. "Please…" it whispered.

I looked outside my cell, but not a guard in sight. With the strength of my fingers, I began to dig. The more I dug, the louder the voice became.

"Let me out, let me out, let me out!"

I dug and dug until I found it; the calaca. A traditional skeleton doll with round black eyes, a broad smile, and wearing a fancy black suit. I held it in my arms like a child. It felt like the most fragile thing in the world.

"What is your name, amigo?" it asked me.

Its lips did not move as if it was speaking into my mind. "Efi. Efi Esqueleto." I responded.

"Ah, Esqueleto. We are the same." it joked. "Who are you?" I asked.

"Emmanuel Mal. I was once a prisoner here until a witch trapped my soul within this calaca. She was quite furious with me after I stole her food, so now I lay here, buried beneath the prison." he explained.

"How did you get buried?" I asked.

"Aye, the man who was here before you. I asked him to help me. But he wanted nothing to do with mágico, so he buried me." he explained.

"Mágico?" I asked.

"Si, mágico is what trapped me. Mágico is what can release me," he said. "What would you have to do?" I asked.

"*You* would have to perform a ritual, releasing my soul from the calaca, and for your service, I would repay you." he said.

"Repay me how?" I asked.

"If you were to help me, I could release you from this cell. You are sentenced to be hanged, no? I could change the sentencing and have you be released." he said.

"How could you do that?" I asked.

"Mágico mi amigo, mágico! I am a man talking to you through a calaca. What more proof do you need?" he says.

"...Alright, I'll do it. What more do I have to lose." I say. "My thoughts exactly!" he says.

All of a sudden, I could hear the noise of approaching footsteps. The guards were returning to their posts.

"Rápido, bury me back in the hole! We will do the ritual tomorrow night!" he says.

As quickly as possible, I place Emmanuel back into the hole and push the dirt back into place. Then I sat where I had put the dirt, so the guards could not see.

I must perform the ritual, and I must escape. I refuse to die here, and I refuse to have my name to be made in jest. I will escape here, Dona, and join you and the family. I will renounce my ways and turn to a life of solitude. I will perform the ritual tomorrow night, set Emmanuel free, and escape this place.

Your brother,
 Efi Esqueleto

October 31, 1848
Mexico City, Mexico

Dear Dona,

I have not been honest with you. The ritual begins at midnight. Rain and thunder roar for the third night in a row, and we have laid out the pentagram. At each point, a different item that I was required to sacrifice: A strand of my hair, a tooth from my mouth, a finger from my hand, an eye from my skull, and an ear from my head, each placed at one of the five points of the star.

And Emmanuel, the calaca, is placed at the center. I have to make this quick, for I am losing much blood. Emmanuel says that he can stop the bleeding once the ritual is complete. But, he did say that he would not be able to repair my appendages. You do what you must to survive. But, one part of this ritual hurts more than physical harm. I must give up the one thing people cling to. They hold onto it, never revealing it, keeping it close to their deaths—the truth. I must reveal the truth of my crimes. Yes, I did kill my wife, Elisa. But the manner of the murder is not as glamorous as I made it out. The truth is, I am a coward. When I discovered Elisa was unfaithful, I did not go barging into town like some cowboy with my gun on my waist looking for blood. I wept like a newborn, and I drank myself to oblivion. After stumbling through the empty streets, I found myself in the tavern. Drinking increasingly till the bartender decided he had enough of my howling. He threw me out of the establishment, weeping all the while about my darling Elisa.

But it seems the town was already privy to my troubles, and I had already appeared to be the butt of the joke.

"Yeah, I hear Elisa's got herself a real man!" says the bartender.

Oh, how the other patrons laugh. At night, in my dreams, that is all I hear.

"Please! What is his name?!" I plead.

"Andres, some drifter who wandered in. I guess Elisa figured she could have some fun!" said the bartender.

I lifted myself off the ground and stumbled down the path. Not sure where I was going. I guess I just needed to walk. I walked for hours until I came across the cabin. The lamps were lit, and I could see into the windows. I saw Elisa. But I did not catch her and Andre making love as I had said. I caught them dancing in the candlelight. It was true love that I could see. I could see it in her eyes, that spark. I remember it well when she loved me. And as time grew, I saw it fade away, and I did nothing about it. She was with me, and that was all that mattered. And if she got mad, stepped out of line, or questioned my love for her, some physical persuasion would be necessary. But with this man, the fire was rekindled. And I hated him for it. I stumbled to the front door and began to bang on it. "Elisa! Open up!" I screamed. I knocked and banged until finally, and I just kicked the door down. Andre was holding her close, clutching his knife, holding it out towards the door. He was protecting her, and this only infuriated me more.

"Go away, Efi! I don't need you anymore." she screamed.

"Like hell! How could you betray me, mi amore?! Are you, not my wife?! Am I, not your provider?! Your protector?!" I screamed, still drowsy from the alcohol.

"But you are none of those things! Maybe once, but not anymore. Not with the beatings and the screaming. I only married you out of pity, Effi. You were weak then, and you still are. I found myself a real man, and I am staying. I hate you!!" she screamed.

I should not have done what I did next, but being intoxicated, my mind was blank. I charged toward Elisa, but Andres stepped forward, and I caught the end of his blade. He stabbed so deep that it stayed inside me when he let go. He backed away, and I fell to the ground. With a wave of anger in me like no other, I pulled the dagger from my stomach and started slashing it at Andres and slashing in every direction, not caring for what I may hit. He dodges my cuts, afraid for his own life. I go to stab him in the gut, and with a quick reaction, he moves out of the way, creating a clear path to Elisa. The knife enters between her ribs, and the blood begins pouring out. In the haze of it all, I hurt the one thing I was trying to protect. She lay gasping on the floor, and Andres rushed to her side. I just stood there and stared at my handiwork. The tears came again, dear sister, not just from me but also from Andres. He held her in his arms, held her tightly, and wept.

"...We met several years ago, Efi. This is not my first time passing through here. When I first arrived, I met her at the tavern, and I fell in love at first sight. But she was married to you and unhappy nonetheless. So we met in secret when you were drunk. And ever since that night, we have been writing love letters to each other. Tonight...I was going to ask her to run away with me. We could've started a new life away from this place...away from you. But it is over." he said in defeat.

"No, not yet." I said as I raised the knife into the air.

I must have stabbed him over a hundred times. By the time it was over, the sun was already rising. I was cold, so I lit a fire in the cabin and waited for...well, I'm not sure what I was waiting for. God's wrath, perhaps? Four officers on horseback came riding up to the cabin and said the townsfolk informed them of a crazy drunk looking to kill his wife. I guess they found it. The moral of this story, Dona is that Elisa was not the problem, neither was Andres or the alcohol; it was myself. I have been a coward all my life. I was too afraid to leave when you and the family left, I was so afraid to lose my wife that I forgot to be there for her, and I was so afraid of Andres being right. That I killed him and Elisa in cold blood. I lost everything that night, and it was all my fault. That is my confession. The ritual can be completed now that it is written for God and all to see. That last part of my soul that needed to be separated from me; was the truth. I have given you the truth and laid myself bare, and in return, I beg for your forgiveness. At five o'clock tomorrow, I am scheduled to be taken to the gallows pole, I shall either leave there a free man, or I will be going in a box. Either way, I love you, sister, and hopefully, when this grand illusion we call life is over, I will see you at the gates of heaven. May God forgive me.

With love, Efi

November 1, 1848

México City, México

Quierda Dona,

It was on a beautiful morning like this when I first realized I was trapped within the doll. I am pleased to tell you that the ritual was a success. Well...a success for me, to be specific. See, I forgot to mention to your brother that for my soul to be released, a soul must be replaced inside the calaca. Your brother's soul was perfect. Depraved, broken, and weak. So now, my soul rests in his body. I assure you he is perfectly fine, and I buried him back in the ground where I was placed. He will rest there until another unlucky man gets placed inside that cell. Everything I told him was true. A witch trapped me inside the calaca after stealing her food, and I have been trapped there for far too long indeed. It was like a nightmare to be buried alive and unable to die. But it has certain advantages when trapped between the land of the dead and the living. There are many exciting people in the spirit realm, people willing to help a poor soul like me and people who know witchcraft. They helped me devise a ritual to break my bonds and release me into the world. I just needed the right person at the right time. Día de Los Muertos is the only time during the year when the veil between the dead and the living is paper thin. Only then could someone, your brother, perform the ritual and release me. I tell you this to let you know that what I did to your brother was not personal. After all, you do what you must survive. Although, if you do not mind me saying, it would seem like I am doing you a favor. Your brother was one piece of work, wasn't he? Anyway, I suppose we will never see each other, although it won't be hard to miss.

How many men with one missing eye, tooth, finger, and ear do you know? I plan on spending the rest of my days in a cabin somewhere. Somewhere far away from México City and certainly somewhere far away from you. Oh yes, I indeed was able to procure your brother's escape. It is such a shame he will not be able to enjoy it himself. You're welcome to grab him if you wish, or you could let him rot there. Or, if you're feeling lucky…you can always find me. Better yet, maybe *I* will find you.

Yours truly
Emmanuel Mal

The Last Sin Eater

They hand me my groat and allow me to enter the room. He lay there on the bed, too young. The boy had been suffering from a bad case of scarlet fever...like my own children. He passed in his sleep. I take my post, sitting on the small stool before the body. I stare at the boy and try to hold back my tears. I grab the bread on his chest and begin to eat it. The bread has soaked up all the sins the boy has left behind. And that is where I come in. I eat the bread, taking upon myself all of the sins. He did not get to make his last rites, so his sin stayed with him. The family pays me a small fee to ensure this little boy makes it to heaven. Of course, I do not know many children who need absolving of sin. But it is the tradition, and the holy book speaks of original sin and how it has been passed down since Adam and Eve, including children. Still, just because the book says it does not make it fair. I finish the bread and move on to the ale, which has been poured into a wooden bowl. All of this, mind you, is the first bit of food that I have eaten in 2 days. But the dead are never in short supply in Wales, and sin-eaters are always in demand. I set the bowl back down on the nightstand. I stand up and say the words I have said thousands of times by now:

"I give easement and rest now to thee, dear boy, that ye walk not down the lanes or in our meadows. And for thy peace, I pawn my own soul. Amen."

I make the sign of the cross, and then I make my leave. As I exit the home, the family is waiting outside for me. But not with thankful tidings or displays of gratitude. I am greeted by a broom handle to the shoulder and a rock thrown at my stomach. See, as much in demand as

sin-eaters are, we are shunned by the community that desires us. As they say, God has a particular sense of humor.

They scream at me:

"Out of here, witch!"

"Take your sin and begone!" "Drunks and infidels, the lot of you!"

These are just words, but they say more about the people than they do me or other

sin-eaters. Sin-eaters are not a particularly sought-after profession. A job for the poor, the needy, and the outcasted. And like all things in society, they shun those who are dealt poor hands and praise those who had an ace up their sleeve the whole game. I go through the crowd, escaping the onslaughts of threats, and back onto the road.

The town of Ratlinghope lies within the lands of Shrewsbury. A farming community tucked away from the rest of the industrial world. The rolling green hills stretch as far as the eye can see, and the smell of nature surrounds you. We have had a bit of a resurgence in Christianity, but even with that, more and more seem to be turning away from the faith. I suppose that is why my services are needed and shunned simultaneously. I live on the outskirts of town, away from everyone, only making my way in to buy supplies or when required. I have repeated this process since 1870, for the last 36 years, since my wife and children died of scarlet fever when I was 39. I was a farmer back then and was content to stay so. But when they died, life became meaningless.

I felt a need to suffer like their deaths were somehow my fault. A punishment dealt out to me by God himself for some indiscretion that I have since lost memory of. I thought perhaps it might do some good. To take my pain and use it for the betterment of the community. And so, I took up the old tradition passed down by my people, the sin eater. I take upon the sins of those passed on from this world, just like Jesus Christ himself. I carry it with me everywhere I go until death. Where I will meet…well, that I am not sure of. I suppose hell, but I am performing a task of God so that heaven might have its place for me. This has never been a sure thing of the sin eaters. It is an old tradition, forgotten and unpracticed since the 1830s when I was a child, mind you. The meaning has been lost, and the practice is outdated, but people are fond of tradition.

As I walk, I can feel it; the sin. As I said, I carry it with me everywhere, and what a heavy burden it is. Over 100 rituals performed have I, and the load gets added each time. I have been unable to stand up straight for decades, my spine curved from the weight. I can feel it in my shoulders and neck each morning, and my legs always have soreness. I have not been a farmer for quite some time, but I remember after a long day of bailing hay, herding my sheep and cow, and harvesting the crops, feeling the same sort of soreness all over. My body strained from a hard day's work, only now there is no hard work to be had. The sin has taken its toll, and I may not be able to do this for much longer. But God works in mysterious ways. I fear my punishment may last much longer than I would like. Punished for what? I still cannot say.

I begin to pass the local church and stop from my route to make my way inside. The pastor has a fondness for me. He disapproves of my profession and is supposed to condemn and cast me out, but he understands my pain. So he lets me on, as long I do not bother any. Generally, I do not. But on this particular day, I am feeling quite bothersome. I enter the old wooden church, dilapidated by time. I approach the priest standing in front of the pedestal. He is reading the bible, no doubt preparing for this afternoon's funeral of the poor boy. I sit at one of the pews and begin my daily prayer.

"Hello there, how nice to see you again." says the priest.

"You as well, Father." I respond. Father Mathias and I have been in this community since we were small boys and used to be in school together. Oh, we were never friends mind you, but we got along just fine. But now, I see Father Mathias more than anyone else.

"If you keep coming in here this often, the people will want me to shun you out, seriously this time." says Father Mathias.

"When do they ever want me anywhere? " I ask.

"In the meantime, "*If you declare with your mouth, "Jesus is Lord," and believe in your heart that God raised him from the dead, you will be saved. For it is with your heart that you believe and are justified, and it is with your mouth that you profess your faith and are saved.*"
-Psalm 51

Father Mathias stands over me, performing the sign of the cross. I look up at him, like a child at their father. My hands clasped together, I listen and say the words under my breath. He prays for me, prays for my forgiveness, prays for my sins, and prays for my family. He finishes and heads back to the podium. I stand up and make my way out of the church.

"I don't suppose you could save some food for me after the funeral?" I ask before I leave.

He looks offended, as maybe he should be. But he has more important things to worry about than an old sinner like me. With a nod and a slight breath, he says, "Sure."

And with that, I take my leave.

***

The body of a beautiful woman lies before me. At 25, she is taken too early from this world. Dark brown hair and as pale as the first winter snow. She reminds me of my wife. Like the boy, she did not have her last rites, and I must save her. Gossip in town mentioned she was a witch, consorting with devils and the like. I pay no mind to it. People are hard on things they do not understand. And besides, witch or not, a man has to eat, and I have not eaten in several days. I eat the bread and drink the wine placed upon her body, and I can feel the sin entering me, going down my throat, and sitting in my stomach like undigested cheese. And with the ritual complete, I begin to say the prayer.

"I give easement and rest now to thee-"

"Do not speak another word!" said a voice in the darkness.

Startled, I open my eyes and look around the room to find the source of the voice. In the past, I have had angry family members interrupt my prayer in protest. They do not like this "witchcraft" and wish to stop it. Only to have another family member escort them out of the room, allowing me to finish. I never truly felt like I was in danger in all those times, except for this. The hairs on my neck stand up, my heart begins to race, and I can truly feel the presence of evil in my soul. I look to the dark corners, the doorway, and the window, and no one can be seen. I look under the bed, and there it is. A demon. Skinny to the bone, small horns, red skin, and black eyes. He lay on the floor under the bed in the fetal position.

"Do not finish your prayer, sin eater, or I shall release the wrath of hell onto you!" he yells at me in anger.

I shout Luke 11:14:

"Jesus was driving out a demon that was mute. When the demon left-"

"Oh, bite your tongue, sin-eater! I am not to be trounced by the lord's words." the demon cries.

I fall backward on the floor and push myself up against the wall. I grab my cross and hold it up in the air at the demon, my hand shaking furiously.

"What do you want, hellspawn? Have you come for this woman's soul? Leave her be! Let her join the lord in peace!" I scream.

"Yes, I have come for this woman's soul. For we are in love, and I have come to bring her to hell, where we can be together forever." he says solemnly.

"You mean to tell me the rumors are true? This woman was a witch?" I ask. "Jezabelle. Her name is Jezabelle. She is a good woman, a beautiful soul. To good for

your lord and the people of this village. She accepted us, my kind, for who we are, and in turn, we accepted her. All the other witches danced around the fire naked during the black sabbath. Yes, there are more witches in your village sin eater, they are everywhere, and they do not go down quietly. Regardless, they were all dancing and summoned us, the demons of hell. They wanted to…"consort" with us, and consort we did. I locked eyes with Jezabelle. She was the fairest of them all. Oh, how could she want me? I am not strong or smart; I am a lesser demon unfit to rule or conquer. But she saw something in me. What it was, I am not sure. But we have been close ever since. Never returning to hell, I stayed by her side, helping her with her witchcraft, falling in love ever so slowly. Until the day she passed, she had scarlet fever. We tried everything, but it seems God had other plans. It seems he was willing to kill such a beautiful thing so it would not fall into the "wrong hands," as you would put it. Well...I have come to take her back." explained the demon.

I see empathy in his eyes, a genuine concern for the well-being of this beautiful creature. I believe that he truly does love her. But I must now allow myself to be tempted. This is all part of the demon's trickery. Demons are notorious liars who will say whatever is necessary to gain your trust and have their way with you.

"I cannot allow you to do that. Even if your words are true, you will condemn this woman to an eternity of torment. And since she is dead and has no say in the matter, I must send her to the lord." I explain.

"Who appointed you to choose her fate if she has no say? Let her rise from the dead and speak her mind if she has no say!" screams the demon.

"It is God's say! And he shall have this creature return to the kingdom of heaven!" I scream.

I shout Luke 11:14, and I finish it.

"Jesus was driving out a demon that was mute! When the demon left, the man who had been mute spoke, and the crowd was amazed!"

As I shout the words, I hold out my cross. The demon squirms and shutters, yelling and screaming. Steam begins to rise from his flesh, my words are burning him, and he is terrified of the cross. I shout the words over and over again. His flesh is searing off, and he is screaming in agony, falling to the floor. He looks like nothing more than de-skinned cattle. Only muscle and bone remain. Twitching in pain, he crawls into a darkened corner of the room. Whimpering and crying, he manages to say something.

"Jezabelle, my love, I am sorry." he says.

Then, he is gone. Fading into the darkness, back into hell. I cannot believe it. The poor, old sin eater has cast the demon out of hell…and no one was around to witness it! But alas, I am in service to God, not the people. I stand in utter shock, waiting to see if anything else will happen. But it remains silent, and the air is still. The smell of sulfur vanishes. It is replaced with fresh flowers. I catch my breath and laugh in utter amazement at my triumph.

I return to Jezabelle and look upon her face. I am almost thankful that she has passed on, unable to witness the horror that almost befell her. Spending an eternity in hell is no laughing matter, and spending it with an obsessive demon is not funny. Again, I am reminded of my wife and my children. Sometimes I feel grateful that they were spared from the rest of this existence. God is good, but how good is he? If the demon had anything of value to say, it is that God does take away the beauty from this world, and it seems to hold no value whatsoever. God's plan is ever mysterious.

I stand over Jezabelle, and I finish the prayer.

"I give easement and rest now to thee, dear woman, that ye walk not down the lanes or in our meadows. And for thy peace, I pawn my soul. Amen."

I make the sign of the cross, and I begin to leave the room. "My love…" says a voice raspy voice.

I turn around, afraid for my life. My first thought is that the demon has returned, and he wants to take his revenge. But from some twisted magic, some sacred witchcraft, I watch Jezabelle slowly rise from the bed and step down, towering above us. Her skin is still just as pale, her black hair hangs down, and her blue eyes glisten in the afternoon sun. Her face was calm, and no emotion could be seen. She is a living corpse!

"Oh, bless me! Jezabelle! The Lord has allowed us to speak!" I say.

"Yes. He has granted me the gift to see my family one last time and to thank you for blessing me." she says.

"Well, child, that is hardly necessary-" I begin to say.

"However, that is not how I wish to spend my final moments here on Earth. I came here to tell you that what you did was wrong. What the demon said was true, we were in love, and I had wished to go to hell." says Jezabelle.

I stare in disbelief, and the words pass through like daggers.

"No! NO! It cannot be! It is another trick. Lies! LIES! Jezabelle, this demon has tricked you and cannot possibly love you. God is the only true one who loves you and can save you. I can save you." I proclaim.

"Poor old fool. Not powerful enough to save his own family, he must try to save the world if he can. You cannot bring your family back, and neither can God. They are gone, and you are alone. God does not care about us, and neither does the devil. All they care about is their war and who is the superior. God and Lucifer treat their followers well but are a means to an end.

Pawns in the game at large." said Jezabelle.

"Then why have you joined the devil if neither care about us? Why not join the ranks of God, where at least you will live in prosperity? And not in eternal damnation?" I ask

"At first, I joined with the dark forces out of spite of this world. I renounced God and all his creations. And when I met with this demon, I thought I would be him as another rebellious act. But then I fell in love with him until I was forever his, and he was mine. And that is when I realized that there is no good or bad. There are no winners, and there are no losers. We paint ourselves how we wish to paint and seek to destroy those not painted the same color. No matter the side, we are all just trying to survive. You have chosen your side, Richard Munslow, and there is honor in that. But the next time you decide to involve yourselves in the affairs of others, I hope you will think of me and the love you destroyed. Goodbye." she said.

And with that, she was gone. Fading into the light to join the ranks of heaven.

On the way out, the mother hands me my groat. I take it, turn it around and inspect it as if it was foreign. I take the mother's hand and place the groat back into her palm.

"That is unnecessary, ma'am, for I have just decided that this will be my last day as a sin eater. Good day." I say.

I exit the house and head back to the church. I sure hope that Father Matthias saved me some food from the funeral. I feel it will be the last meal I will ever eat.

A Song for A Cowboy

The sun and moon are chieftains of the sky, and the stars are their children. But the sun likes to eat the stars, so they flee whenever he enters the sky. The moon, however, loves to play with her children, and they rejoice and shine whenever she is in the sky.

"Drink that rot gut, drink that rot gut, Drink that red-eye, boys

It don't make a damn wherever we land, We hit her up for joy."

And on this night, the moon and the stars are brighter than ever. They shine a spotlight onto a lone man sitting on a log by a campfire in the wastelands of New Mexico and singing songs into the dark. To his left, his horse is tied up on a post he placed into the ground, and to his right, his dinner. Beans in a can and an empty plate of bacon. He pokes and prods the fire with a short stick, stoking it, keeping it as bright as the moon and stars.

"We've lived in the saddle and ridden trail, Drink old Jordan, boys,

We'll go whooping and yelling, we'll all go a-helling; Drink her to our joy."

After a long day's ride, it's good to sit by the fire and sing your cares away, especially when you are a man on a mission. But even a lone rider such as this needs friends, even when they come from the most unexpected places. Out from the dark, amongst the New Mexico desert plains, another voice begins to sing along. It's beautiful, what the Italians call a Leggero Baritone. It scares the devil out of our poor man.

"Whoop-ee! drink that rot gut, drink that red nose, Whenever you get to town;

Drink it straight and swig it mighty, Till the world goes round and round!"

It's the moment he's been waiting since he started this journey. Quickly, out from his satchel, he grabs a bottle of whiskey. He pours the beans from his can and fills a little whiskey. Crouching and shuffling across the ground, he places the can at the firelight's edge. He then sits back on his log and continues to sing.

"As I walked out one morning for pleasure, I met a cowpuncher a jogging along;

His hat was throwed back and his spurs was a jingling, And as he advanced he was singing this song."

As if on cue, like an actor taking the stage, out steps our subject. A giant rabbit, the size of a bulldog, with tall, pointy antlers. A Jackalope. He hops up to the can of whiskey, smelling it, curious. Looking over at the cowboy, he seems preoccupied, looking deep into the fire. Out of sight, he stands upright like a human, grabbing the can with his paws and taking a big swig of the midnight liquid. After a few gulps, the clicking can be heard. He knows it all too well. The clicking like a rattlesnake taunting its prey, a warning that smoke and fire shall breach the flesh and leave a hole in your gullet. The Jackalope looks up to find the cowboy pointing the large metal wand toward his head.

"Try to hop away, little creature, and dis here 6 iron will plant one right between your pretty little antlers." gruffed the cowboy.

The cowboy set the trap, and boy, it sprung. He had been traveling for three nights to find this Jackalope. And every night, lighting up that fire and singing into the dark. It's common knowledge that Jackalope loves to sing along with a singing cowboy. And better known is that Jackalopes love whiskey. It's about time this infernal beast showed up, this cowboy doesn't drink, but he was told it was good whiskey. He felt like it might have been going to waste.

"Oh please, do not set me ablaze. My father had a run-in with your kind a few years back, and his face was nearly melted off from your flaming spell. And I don't wish to inherit his looks." said the Jackalope.

"Well, I'll be, the beast speaks! Dem fellers at the reservation mentioned nothing bout that. But, it sure will make dis a whole lot easier to negotiate." said the cowboy.

In a moment of bravery, the Jackalope speeds toward the cowboy. He could feel the rabbit's large feet thumping, smacking up a dust bowl of sand and dirt. Antlers first and aimed at the cowboy's legs. The cowboy shoots, but the thing moves pretty damn fast. Fortunately, the cowboy remembered to put his steel plates on his shins, a known technique when dealing with Jackalopes. It smashes against the plates, chipping the tip of its antlers, the weakest point. The cowboy quickly grabs the Jackalope by his antlers. It kicks and wiggles in the air, but it is completely helpless.

"Now, why'd you have to go and do a thing like that? I almost killed ya, and seein' as how I've been looking for ya', killing ya' sure would've created a lot of wasted time." said the cowboy.

"I'm sorry, sir, please forgive me. But, I do truly despise your race and wish to see you all banished from this land. I do, from time to time, forget that you were able to oppress for a reason. Your aptitude for violence is truly remarkable." said the jackalope.

"Well, that there is just the human condition. It can't be helped. Now, I'm going to tie you up here on Sally Joe, my trusty steed. And I want no trouble from ya. I've got a proposition that I think will benefit us both. And if you are willing to hear me out, you might just come out of this unharmed. Sound good?" asked the cowboy.

"Oh yes, sir, very much so!" replied the jackalope.

The cowboy tied up the jackalope. First, its front paws tied them behind its back. And then its back paws. He tied it up like you would a regular person and then sat it up on the horse. The strange rabbit waited patiently, afraid for its life but also curious. No human in its long and supernatural life span had wanted to communicate with it. And none especially wanted to make a deal with it. It stared at the cowboy, grizzled, scruff on his face, wrinkles so deep you could fall asleep in them, salt and pepper hair covered by his cowboy hat, tall, if not aided by his cowboy boots. Jeans, a vest, and a button-up shirt tucked in. And what cowboy is complete without his Winchester rifle and a hunting knife attached to the hip? The cowboy pours himself a cup of coffee, which has been brewing on the fire for some time now. And then, he refills the can with more whiskey. He sits beside the log and sits down to enjoy his coffee.

"May I ask?..." said the jackalope. "You may not." said the cowboy.

"Are you going to drink that whiskey you have set aside?" asked the Jackalope. "I gave up drinking long ago." replied the cowboy.

"Oh, then, might I perhaps-" began the Jackalope.

"You might. You might, perhaps. Ifn' you agree to my terms." said the cowboy. "...I'm all ears...Or antlers." giggled the jackalope.

The cowboy, stone-faced, clearly lacking a sense of humor, takes a swig of his coffee, grabs the can of whiskey, and stands up. Lifting his pants for a quick adjustment, he walks to the jackalope. The jackalope can barely sit still, licking its lips and wagging its tail. It leans its head forward, trying to get the smell of that dizzying elixir. Eye-level, the cowboy stares deep into the eyes of the jackalope. Eyes are the windows into the soul, they say, and the cowboy was looking for...well, he didn't know what he was looking for. Anything, I guess.

"So here's the thing strange rabbit, Imma shoot straight with ya. I have a lady, and she's fallen ill. The doctor ain't any help. I have tried every medicine the general store will offer me, I even tried the natives here, and nothing seems to be helping." said the cowboy.

"...I'm sorry." said the jackalope, genuinely concerned.

"One night, I'm chatting with the natives, and they tell me about an animal that might be able to help me: a mystical animal, an animal resembling a large rabbit and with horns like a deer. And supposedly, this animal's milk has magical healing properties. Now I'm not one to believe in fairy tales. But what choice do I have? So I grabbed my gear and set out to find this rabbit with horns." explained the cowboy.

"Technically, they are called antlers but..." said the jackalope.

Again, the cowboy did not find this amusing.

"Choice is your's little one. You can give me your milk, or you can die here." offered the cowboy.

The jackalope looked down in thought, afraid of what he knew he had to say.

"I am afraid I am not going to be of much use. I am a male and cannot produce the milk you seek. I am sorry." said the jackalope.

"Well then, you're going to lead me to your… "people" and bring me a gal whose milk is the best of ya'll." said the cowboy.

"Oh no, I cannot do that, sir. I would not give up one of my kin. And they would not do the same. They would rather die."

The cowboy lifted his rifle and pointed it in the creature's direction. "I can certainly do that for them." threatened the cowboy.

"Oh, I have no doubt. But I think you need to ask yourself, dear cowboy, how long do you expect to last against the full might of my tribe? Your silly metal pads cannot protect from a full onslaught. You might kill a few of us, but there is no doubt we would be the victorious ones." explained the jackalope.

He was right, and the cowboy knew it. "…Shit." said the cowboy. He turned away from the jackalope, not to show it defeat, not to show it the tears beginning to form in his eyes. Maybe this was it—the end of the road.

"The wife is not going to be happy with this...goddamnit!" yelled the cowboy, his voice choked up.

It was here that the jackalope sensed something different about the cowboy. A man with an aptitude for violence, but with purpose, with heart. He thought of himself and if he were in a similar situation with one of his lovers. In fact, he had known many a jackalope who had found death in defense of loved ones from humans. Would he have done the same?

"But...I do know of another way." said the jackalope.

The cowboy turned around quickly, eyes widened, staring intensely at the jackalope.

Eager to hear its tale.

"There is a place, 4 days travel with your horse. We call it The Untouched, a place left undisturbed by the colonizers. The last oasis of the desert. The Untouched plays host to some of the rarest and most magical flowers on this Earth. One of those flowers, Sanus Exotica, is known for its healing properties. I have seen it cure all ailments, from a wounded leg caused by a bear trap to polio that had constrained a poor man to a wheelchair. I watched him eat the flower from the ground and then, magically, walk right up to his wife and children, who had watched the whole thing. Hope exists at The Untouched."

The cowboy was left speechless. Hope. That's all that he had. He rushed to the log to grab the whiskey can and returned to the jackalope. He held the can in its face, almost like an offering. The jackalope, intoxicated by the smell, looked to be in pure ecstasy.

"If you can take me there, I promise you, not only will I let you go, but I will give you *all* the whiskey you can handle." the cowboy offered.

"Well...Whiskey later, yes...but-" Without another word, the cowboy grabbed his hunting knife and untied the front paws. Though annoyed, he needed trust from the jackalope, a small token of gratitude. He attempts to hand over the can of whiskey gently, but the jackalope, gripped by compulsion, grabs the can from him and begins to chug the whiskey. Sloshing out of the can, leaving stains around its mouth, the droplets falling. Some of it gets on Sally Joe, causing her to shiver and shake, knocking the jackalope to the ground. Face flat in the dirt, back legs tied, it lies in defeat. The cowboy, back at the log, finishes his coffee and stares into the fire with a longing that could shake trees. Hope has filled this cowboy's boots, and he's soaking it in. "Oh heavens, that

is great stuff! Soooo…vat du I cul you zir cowwwboi?"
drunkenly said

the jackalope.

"No names. Cowboy is fine. Boy, for a creature that
loves whiskey, you sure don't know how to handle it."
said the cowboy.

"Ah, yes, weyll…I dut rink dat ofnnn.." droned the
jackalope.

And just like that, the jackalope fell asleep. Snoring,
drooling, lying in the dirt, the cowboy stares at it. "It
almost looks cute." he thinks to himself. As the fire dims,
the stars become brighter. They are playing with the
moon, so intensely before the sun arrives. "I wonder if
jackalopes make good pets?"

***

The stars have disappeared, and the sun has risen,
angry that it did not catch a single star. During their
journey, the sun did not let up. It beats down hard, and
there is no rest from it. Four days ride, and two days in,
the cowboy and the jackalope are already exhausted.
Along their journey, many a restless night, and they have
seen many horrors. Indian reservations were burnt to the
ground, and American soldiers looked through the refuse.

Bodies piled like wood to the flames, each with their own story. Men, women, children, it made no difference. The men were stealing supplies, food, medicine, and goods to trade. Everything else was thrown about or thrown to the fire. Some men were gutting the freshly hunted animals of the day, deer and raccoons.

"I think I am going to be sick." said the Jackalope. "Don't even think about it." said the cowboy.

"How can you allow this? How can you all come here and do this?" said the Jackalope. "I came here to live a life away from these folks. This ain't none of my concern." said the cowboy.

"Yes, it is. It is all of our concern. You will see in due time." said the Jackalope.

The cowboy didn't know what the creature meant, and he did not ask him. They moved on.

***

The jackalope sits behind the cowboy, panting like a dog. Tongue exposed and eyes half closed, it droops forward, trying to cover itself in the shadow of the cowboy. Covered in sweat, the cowboy wipes his forehead, and his only sanctuary is the shade cast by the brim of his hat. The cowboy checks the road—same as before, nothing but sand, rocks, and the angry sun. Even Sally Joe, the toughest, most loyal steed, begins to slow her pace. Time moves slowly, boredom creeping in, and the jackalope attempts to make conversation.

"So…cowboy…may I ask about your girl?" said the jackalope.

The cowboy, silent as the grave. Clearly, he is not interested in the musing of some fairyland creature. But even a cowboy, who sits in the loneliness of the range, and who rides for many moons, gets bored from time to time.

"…She's a school teacher." said the cowboy.

"Ah, a learned woman, eh? Where did you two meet?" asked the jackalope.

"Well…the town was having a ball one Christmas. I was sitting at the bar, and she approached me. She said, "Now, what could be at the bottom of that glass, that's more important than Christmas Eve?" Oh, I was ready to give her a piece of my mind, but when I saw how beautiful she was, hoo boy, I swear my heart skipped a beat. I told her, "Well, ma'am, I am looking for the secret to life." And then she said, "Well, sugar, this is your lucky day." She grabbed my hand, and we danced all night. I walked her home, and on the way there, I asked her,

"Now, what made you want to bother little old me?" And she said, "Even a cowboy doesn't deserve to be lonely on Christmas?" Then I kissed her. A few months later, I proposed. We'd been together ever since. Three years now."

As the cowboy finished, he heard the faint sound of sniffling. He looked over to find the jackalope with tears in his eyes, wiping them away.

"Oh, I'm terribly sorry, I am a sucker for love stories." said the jackalope.

The cowboy turned back, a little embarrassed. He didn't mean to share so much about himself, but talking about his lady always gets him going. "She sounds wonderful." The cowboy changes the subject quickly. He is holding the jackalope hostage. After all, he cannot show weakness.

"Anyway...I don't suppose jackalopes have spouses." said the cowboy.

"Oh, not really. We have a beautiful but intense dance routine that we must perform to attract females. Once done correctly, and after several attempts, we are approached by said female, and we mate. We usually create a dozen or so offspring in a matter of weeks. I once sired two dozen offspring. Now that was the talk of my tribe for months." explained the jackalope.

"Well...we're still working on one." said the cowboy. Suddenly, Sally Joe stops and sits down on her stomach.

"Why have we stopped?" asked the jackalope.

The cowboy gets off Sally Joe and begins to rummage through the bags. "She's exhausted. She needs a break." said the cowboy.

He rifles through his things until he finds the canteen of water. He takes a swig and tilts the canteen so the water begins pouring out and Sally Joe can drink some water. The cowboy tosses the canteen over to the jackalope.

"Where to now, rabbit?" asked the cowboy.

"Jackalope, not rabbit, and if we continue East the way we're going, we should be able to reach The Untouched in the next two days." said the jackalope.

"You sure there isn't a faster way, rabbit? " said the cowboy. "Jacka-...no, there isn't." responded the jackalope.

The cowboy looked across the open terrain of sand and rocks. Patches of green grass stand out against copper and grey sand. Mesas stand tall against the horizon. Large rock formations that have stood since the dawn of time.

The sun sits above the mesa's flat top, almost like it holds the sun, making sure it heats the valley. Some stand as tall as the heavens, some stand alone, and some stand in groups. One of the groups of mesas seems to stretch on for miles and look like a passageway, creating a canyon.

"What about through the canyon? We should be able to cut through the entire desert in a day." said the cowboy.

"Oh no, bandits and miners hide themselves up in those mesas. They tear into the mesa, looking for gold and stealing from passersby's who come through the path." explained the jackalope.

"Gold?" asked the cowboy.

"Legend tells of a thundergod that resides within the canyon. Dark clouds form above, yet the rest of the sky remains cloudless. The clouds contain a dance of lighting and a continuous roaring of thunder. And the rain. Days of rain, yet only over the canyon. And the water seems to absorb into the mesa itself. There should be life, grass, or something. Only death remains there. And ever since you colonizers started exploiting the land, it has only become worse." explained the jackalope. It takes a swig from the canteen.

The cowboy stares at the entrance to the canyon. The irony stabbed him in the heart. The path to salvation is also the path to death. Then again, he was never one to listen to his brain. Or to jackalopes, for that matter. The cowboy grabs the canteen from the jackalope, mid-drink, and packs it up.

"You ready, Sally Joe?" asked the cowboy.

He hops back onto the horse, the jackalope quickly moving over to make room. "Cowboy?" asked the jackalope.

But he did not respond. Without another word, he steers Sally Joe towards the mesas, towards the entrance of doom.

"Cowboy, please. Your wife won't be able to get the herbs she needs if you're dead." said the jackalope.

"My wife might be dead by the time I return. If this lessens our journey by a day and gives my wife a chance to live, I'm sure as hell willing to die for that. We ride to the canyon. Unless you don't want to and I can just shoot you right here." threatened the cowboy. The jackalope went silent.

***

They stand at the entrance to the canyon. The cowboy looks on in bravery while the jackalope cowers with its tail between its legs.

"We could still turn back?" said the jackalope.

Without a glance, the cowboy clicks his tongue, and Sally Joe clip-clops forward. As they rode on, they took in their surroundings. They couldn't see the top of the canyon. If anyone were watching them, they surely wouldn't be able to know. They also noticed the sky beginning to dim, which was strange considering how bright and sunny it was moments ago. The cowboy digs his spurs into Sally Joe's sides, signaling her to pick up the pace. As she does, her steps begin to echo through the canyon. The sound of a drummer making a sweet rhythm makes a man want to sing…or a jackalope. Not even a few miles into the canyon, the jackalope can't help but sing himself a song.

"As I walked out one morning for pleasure, I met a cowpuncher a jogging along;

His hat was throwed back and his spurs was a jingling, And as he advanced he was singing this song."

The sweet Baritone reverberates across the canyon, echoing back like a chorus. The cowboy doesn't seem too interested. In fact, he looks a bit worrisome.

"Might not be good to sing right now on account of those bandits you were so worried about." said the cowboy.

"If we're going to die, I am going out with a song, thank you very much." replied the jackalope.

The sky began to ring with the roar of thunder and the sting of lighting. And the more the jackalope sang, the worse it seemed to get.

"Yippee Ti Yi Yo, get along little dogies It's your misfortune and none of my own Yippee Ti Yi Yo get along little dogies

For you know that Wyoming will soon be your home."

Then came the rain. Sudden and hard, it drenches them.

"Member' that thunder god you were talkin' bout? I'm not sure if he likes your singing too much." said the cowboy, uncertainty in his voice.

"What's not to like about my singing? In my colony, I was known as the Jongleur Jackalope, on account that I can sing, dance, and do impress-" the roaring of thunder

81

cut off the jackalope, and then, a powerful bolt of lighting launches itself right next to Sally Joe, causing her to rear up and Whinney the loudest she ever has.

"Woah, girl!" screamed the cowboy.

It scored the Earth, leaving a crater and scorch marks. The jackalope holds on for dear life, clutching onto the cowboy's shirt. The cowboy clutches the reigns tight and whips them hard.

"Ride, girl, ride!" screamed the cowboy.

Sally Joe takes off, the rain splashing hard against their face. As they speed away, lighting rains down, aimed sporadically, behind and in front of them, always barely missing them. Loud as can be, they shake the ground, leaving smoke and the smell of burning with them. Dodging and weaving left and right, they miss the lighting bolts, too close for comfort. Just ahead, they can see the exit to the canyon, home free.

"I can see the exit! Almost there!" screamed the cowboy.

The cowboy whips the reigns, and Sally Joe dashes off like she's been possessed by the devil himself.

They are about to make it. They're close, right at the exit. The clouds only circle the canyon, but you can see the sunset shining through at the exit, beckoning toward them. Dodging left and right, the lightning comes behind them and barely misses. It's loud, and one shock would surely kill them, but there's no stopping now. The cowboy made a promise to his love, and he intends to keep it. But fate has a funny way of sneaking up on us. A loud boom echoes through the canyon. If not for the smell of gun smoke wafting through the air, one would assume it was another lightning bolt. The cowboy goes down. He's been hit. The jackalope lands next to him, a bit winded but still intact.

"Cowboy, you alright?" asked the jackalope.

It looked over to see its companion holding his right shoulder. Something had grazed him. It could see by the expressions on his face and the pool of blood that began to form around him that the cowboy was in intense pain.

"No, I'm not fine! I just got shot! And where's Sally Joe?" said the cowboy.

Sally Joe had become startled and ran down the valley, heading toward the exit. By the time they looked over, she was nothing but a tiny spec of paint on the canvas of the landscape.

"So much for your trusty steed." said the jackalope sarcastically. "Nah, she just got spooked, is all. She'll be back." said the cowboy.

They're soaked, the rain never-ending. The rain washes away the blood, winding through the crevasses of the rocks, but the wound is ever-present. Muscle tissue can be seen through the tatters and wears of his shirt.

"Don'tchu move a muscle!" said a voice from above.

The two look up to find three men, holding rifles, standing just over the ridge, their barrels aimed at them. Their overalls are dirt-covered, and a pickaxe hangs from their waists. They are the miners that the jackalope was talking about. The diggers disturbed the thunder god beneath. Or so they say. The cowboy looks to his right, about 2 feet away from him, and sees his rifle on the ground. It was attached to Sally Joe and must've come loose when she took off. The cowboy attempts to reach for it.

"I wouldn't do that if I were you. Chu' ain't supposed to be round here." said the first miner from above.

"If I'm not mistaken, sir, neither are you." responded the jackalope. "Shh! Do you want to get killed?" whispered the cowboy.

"Y'all just go back the way you came, ya hear?" said the second miner. "Ain't happenin' mister." said the cowboy.

The miners cock their rifles.

"He wasn't asking." said the third miner menacingly.

The cowboy is losing blood fast, and they're running out of time. They need to get a move on, or this trip is going to be cut short. The jackalope, without hesitation, gets off the ground and stands up tall and proud on his hind legs. It looks up to the miner, a stern look on its face, and puts his paws behind its back. Then, it begins to sing…again.

"It was on a cold and stormy night I saw and heard an awful sight;

The lightning flashed and thunder rolled Around my poor benighted soul."

"What the hell are you doing, you little…rabbit? What the hell are you?" screamed the first miner. As the song describes, the lighting began to flash again, and the thunder started rolling, the rain getting heavier and heavier.

"I thought I heard a mournful sound Among the groans still lower down, That awful sight no tongue can tell

Is this, — the place called Drunkard's Hell."

The lighting crashes on the ground again, barely missing the jackalope and the cowboy.

But slowly, the lighting begins to crash closer and closer to the miners. It's almost as if the jackalope uses his singing voice to control the lightning.

"Stop that! Stop that right now or I'll shoot!" screamed the first miner. "I thought I saw the gulf below

Where all the dying drunkards go. I raised my hand and sad to tell

It was the place called Drunkard's…HELL!"

Like an opera singer, it holds the final note in a grand finale. And as it does, like a round of applause, a barrage of bolts surrounds the canyon, striking each miner one after the other. It strikes through their hearts, smoke bellowing from their bodies. The first miner's hands are raised to the sky in pain, almost like he is begging his God to give him one final chance. But he falls to the ground, dropping the rifle. As the miner falls, the sky begins to clear, the clouds depart, the thunder and lightning cease, and the sun shines brighter than before. Whatever the jackalope did, it seemed to work. Maybe the thunder god was pleased after all? But no time to think about that.

"Jackalope…" said the cowboy wearily.

The jackalope turned to find the cowboy white as a ghost. He was losing a lot of blood, the wound still gaping.

"It's alright, my friend. I am trained in these sorts of injuries." said the jackalope.

It looks around, seeing if there was anything else that Sally Joe dropped before she took off. Luckily, the canteen lay not far from them. The jackalope took the canteen and poured water onto the wound. Then it tore some of the cowboy's shirt off and wrapped it around the wound tightly.

"Hold this tight. We should be able to reach The Untouched within a day now. If you can hold on till then, I can heal you. But you have to be strong, understood?" asked the jackalope.

"You don't have to explain…nothin' to me…I'm not leaving her behind." said the cowboy in short breaths.

And as if on cue, Sally Joe, the magnificent horse, came galloping back down the valley to her master.

"I told ya…she'd come back." said the cowboy. They packed their things, and gently, the cowboy managed to seat himself up on Sally Joe with the jackalope behind him. They exited the valley, making their way to The Untouched.

***

"No, it can't be." said the jackalope.

They've been riding all night, no sleep. The sun began to rise as they reached The Untouched. But no amount of sunlight could cure what they saw on the horizon. A large, grey tree withered, its life sucked dry by the desert heat. There's a large ravine circling the tree. It was empty, but it had been filled with water at some point. It must've dried up ages ago. Surrounding the base of the tree were dead, wilted flowers. It seems that the settlers of this land were doing more damage than they were aware of. The flower, Sanus Exotica, is all but extinct. Sally Joe slowly made her way up to the tree. Still wounded, the cowboy slumps over, his right arm hanging down. With his left hand, he holds onto the reigns. He barely hangs on to Sally Joe, ready to collapse from the pain. The jackalope, in horror and shock, looks towards the grey tree. As they get closer, the jackalope jumps off Sally Joe and hops over. When he reaches the tree, he kneels, sadness in his voice.

"...No...it's gone...the tree...the flowers...all gone." he said to himself.

He looks up at the withered branches, the dry bark, and its soulless color; the tree is dead, and there's no chance of revival.

"Cowboy, I'm sorry. All is lost." cried the Jackalope.

But it seemed that not all was lost just yet. Tucked way in the dead grass lies a single, solitary purple flower. Sanus Exodus.

"Cowboy! I found it! There's one flower left. We did it!" screamed the jackalope in delight.

…Cowboy?" said the jackalope. But the cowboy did not respond. "Cowboy?" asked the jackalope.

Maybe he was stunned, thought the jackalope. Perhaps he was crying silently as well. Or maybe he left without a word. But when the jackalope turned around, he found the cowboy on the ground. He must've slumped over at some point, the pain too unbearable. Motionless, he lay on the ground, Sally Joe standing over him—his watchful protector.

"No, no, no, no!" screamed the jackalope.

He rushes over to the cowboy and pushes him over onto his back. The cowboy struggles to breathe as he has lost a lot of blood, and the pain from the injury has become unbearable. In short, fast breathes, he tries to speak to the jackalope.

"Jackalope…" said the cowboy.

"It's okay, it's okay, just lay still." said the Jackalope.

"No…promise me…you'll cure her…no matter what…" said the cowboy. "I promise you, she will be cured." said the jackalope.

The cowboy, devoid of strength, raises his hand and points his finger toward Sally Joe. "The pouch…the whiskey…you've earned it…"

The cowboy's arm falls to the ground.

The jackalope looks into his eyes but can find nothing. It can hear the cowboy's breath escaping him…until silence. Not a beat of the heart, sigh of the breath, or blink of the eyes. The cowboy was dead.

***

It's a starless night tonight. The moon is out, but she shines with sadness. The sun has devoured her children. Shaped as a half crescent, she could not muster the strength to complete her form. But she is not the only one that weeps. A woman is in pain in a cabin on the outskirts of a nearby town placed neatly in the desert. She has been sick for the last 2 months, and her husband has left her searching for a cure. She stayed up for many sleepless nights, worrying if her husband would return. Her curly, red hair is oily from a lack of bathing, bags under her eyes, pale as a ghost, with a sickly yellow glow. As she lies in her bed, trying to sleep, she quickly gets up, leans over, and grabs the bucket beside her bed. She vomits all of the disease and bile into that bucket. She wipes the fluid from her mouth and wipes her forehead of sweat. She is tired of this, and she feels she is ready to die.

Out in the darkness, she can hear the clop of hooves approaching her home. She grabs the small oil lamp from her bedside table, her only light source, and moves as quickly as possible to her front door.

"You're back! "You're back! You came back!" she starts to scream.

She opens the door, not to a man, but to an animal. A jackalope was riding a horse and wearing a cowboy hat that sat right between his antlers. She stares with a mixture of amazement and fear. Her first thought was that the sickness had begun to make her hallucinate and that she might enter heaven's gates sooner than she thought. "Hello, ma'am, forgive my intrusion. I don't mean to scare and disturb you in the middle of the night.

But I am a friend of your husband." explained the jackalope.

"What? I- I must be dreaming…the sickness is making me woozy." said the woman. "I assure you, ma'am, I wish you were. You must believe me, ma'am. I'm only here to

help." said the jackalope.

"Well…that is Sally Joe. I would recognize her anywhere. And you do have my husband's hat, and that would be his rifle hanging from Sally Joe. But…what seems to be missing is my husband himself. How do I know you didn't kill him? And that you're here to kill me? I heard that jackalopes are spawns of the devil himself." said the woman.

"Ma'am, I swear to the highest power that I intend you no harm. You see, he recruited me to help him to find a cure for your illness. And well, I'm happy to say, we found it." said the jackalope.

He reaches over to the satchel hanging from Sally Joe and pulls out the bottle of whiskey the cowboy promised him.

"I mixed the cure here, within this bottle of whiskey. Your husband promised it to me but…I think I will try and cut back." said the jackalope. He holds out the bottle for her to grab. She slowly walks over and is about to grab the bottle but hesitates.

"...He's dead, isn't he?" said the woman. The jackalope took off its hat and held it in its lap.

"A man once told me of the woman he loved, who saw a stranger alone on Christmas Eve and gave him the time of day. And they fell in love, despite the tragedies that befall this world.

And this man would do anything to save that love, to preserve it. It gives me hope that humanity has some good left in them." said the Jackalope.

The woman, still with a hesitant look on her face, slowly grabs the bottle of whiskey. "...Thank you. You are a good Jackalope." said the woman.

"I'll be rooting for you, ma'am. I hope to see you again." said the jackalope.

And with a whip of the reigns, Sally Joe turns around and rides off. As it rides away, the sun is slowly beginning to rise. The sun, with a full belly from eating his children, shines brighter than ever before. And you can hear the faint singing of the jackalope.

"I know there's many a stray cowboy Who'll be lost at the great, final sale,

When he might have gone in the green pastures Had he known of the dim narrow trail

I wonder if ever a cowboy

Stood ready for that Judgement Day, And could say to the Boss of the Riders "I'm ready, come drive me away"

Last Wish

The closer Amani arrives, the worse the storm becomes. Even with her burqa, the Arabian sand scratches her face, stings her eyes, and the wind blows her robe. Her silhouette can barely be seen against the raging storm. 7 long nights she has traveled, selling herself to the comforts of strangers and sleeping on the streets. Something not foreign to her but still painful.

She arrives at the entrance to a cave. Buried in the Arabian desert are long-forgotten structures, remnants of forgotten cities filled with false idols. And the storm has awakened it from its ancient slumber, revealing a tall spire reaching the heavens. It appears to be some kind of temple, collapsed and buried in the sands of time. But the infrastructure remains cold and dark. She enters, knowing what she will find. The first real bit of refuge she's had in several days. Inside was nothing but an old ruin filled with lost treasures. Plates, goblets, jewelry, and coins lay about. Anyone else would have snatched these up immediately, but that is not her true purpose. Limestone walls cracked with age, banners of a lost kingdom ripped and torn, and the bones of hundreds lay about the ground. Amani could only imagine what tragedy took place here. Ahead of her lay corridors leading deeper into the temple. From her knapsack, she pulled out a small wooden case. She then looked around the room and found a plank of wood. She then tore off a piece of her robe and wrapped it around the plank. She opened up her small case and grabbed the small amount of flint that lay inside. Scratching against a rock on the ground, she ignited the flint and lit the cloth on the wood aflame. No longer shrouded in darkness, Amani entered deeper into the temple.

Walking deeper into darkness, she looked at the carvings drawn along the temple walls. The first carving depicts a man kneeling before a giant cloud with evil eyes. The second carving

beside it shows the man surrounded by gold and trinkets, the cloud creature lurking in the background. The final carving shows the man dead on the ground, his body twisted and contorted, the cloud creature luring above him. Amani was in the right place, and she had found the home of the Jinn. The Jinn were creatures of smokeless fire with red eyes and a haunting presence. All across the Middle East, legends of the Jinn vary. In Arabia, they say the Jinn can grant you one wish, but you pay a terrible price in return. Very few have ever outsmarted the Jinn, and those that have, receive their place among the gods. Amani wanted no such glory.

She reached the end of the corridor and entered a room. Illuminated by her torchlight, nothing about the room seemed special. Along the walls were the same banners with the symbols of some long-forgotten colony. And at the center of the room was a statue. A king long-forgotten, whose rule indeed brought these people to their demise or at least invited whatever evil lay dormant at their feet. Perhaps the Jinn. The Jinn are responsible for the demise of many cultures—namely, the lost city of Iram, the city of brass. Amani would have liked to believe that she was walking through that fabled city, that she might be welcomed home as an adventurer and gain the respect she well deserved. But this is not a fairy tale.

As she wandered through the empty room, walking straight up to the king's statue, she looked at its face. She lifted her torch, noticing the king's handsome features, exaggerated, of course. Kings are never handsome up close, only in history.

"How lovingly you gaze upon my face?" said a voice.

Startled, she backed away from the statue. Still looking at its face, she realized that its lips were moving. It was speaking to her.

"Now…let me look upon yours." said the voice.

A dark, black smoke began to form around the face. Amani started coughing as the smell of sulfur and burnt wood began to fill the room. The black smoke dropped from the statue and landed on the floor in front of Amani. She immediately turned around and ran.

"Amani!" screamed the voice.

She stopped. Like a magic spell, the creature had frozen her in place with her name.

Torch in hand, she turned slowly, only to find the haunting cloud, black as the cold night, was now in the shape of a man. The man who was carved in stone centuries ago, the forgotten king. Tall, handsome, and clasped in a robe and a crown. But it was a crown of fire, blazing, infernal. And his eyes were a crimson red. He was like a ghost, transparent and haunting. Amani knew this was what she was looking for—the Jinn.

"Hello Amani, I have been waiting for you," said the Jinn. "How do you know my name?" said Amani.

"I know all who seek me, child. I know all. I am the eternal fire." said the Jinn. "I am here to ask for a wish." said Amani.

"As do all who come to me. I can grant you anything you want, just like this king. I once granted him this kingdom and all the riches and power he desired. But his kingdom would be forgotten, and it would all crumble before him. I sure hope he enjoyed it while it lasted." said the Jinn.

The Jinn waved his hand to the bottom of the statue, and Amani noticed for the first time a complete skeleton lay at the bottom of the statue. And at its head was a crown. This was the forgotten king from long ago. Doomed to lie at the monument of his failure as the Jinn laughs at him forever.

"I do not want riches." said Amani.

"If not riches, then what? Perhaps power?" said the Jinn.

"I am poor and forced to sell myself just to survive. I would love nothing more than to rule over those who have taken advantage of me and to bring about a new age of peace and prosperity. But I have seen good, honest people take positions of power, only to see them corrupted. Many have blamed creatures like yourself, but I know better." said Amani.

"So, not riches and not power? Maybe love? Surely you are lonely, given your…profession?" said the Jinn.

"Once, I had a husband. But he left me for another woman of the higher nobility. But with that marriage came a child, a son I love with all my heart. He is waiting for me back home, in the care of my friend. I do not know if she can care for him or if he will even be alive when I return. Life is so fragile, and those without wealth are to live with violence and crime. Someone to care for me and my son and defend us from the horrors of the world would be a wish worth asking. But no, I do not wish for love. For it has brought me nothing but grief." said Amani.

"Then…what do you want, my dear? No wish is too big, nothing is impossible, and anything your heart desires! But as you know…it comes with a price. Wish carefully." said the Jinn.

Amani took a long, deep breath. She cleared her mind, ready for whatever was to come next. She turns around, away from the Jinn. She came all this way to ask him one question, yet she was afraid of the answer. She cannot look at him when he answers. Closing her eyes, she speaks.

"My wish, dear Jinn, is this: I wish to know the true purpose of existence. Is there a divine plan intended for us? Or do we simply just exist? My son asked me this question, and I had no answer. I am not a smart woman, and I am not educated. All I have had is time. Time to think, time to wonder, and time to suffer. My son has suffered, and he has yet to experience this world. Surely, this suffering is for not? Surely he is meant for something greater? There are millions dead in the grave, thousands in pain, and thousands without wealth. You yourself are trapped in this cave. Are we, not all meant for greatness? Or is there nothing? That is why I have come to you, Jinn, to find an answer for my son. And maybe, to give him hope. That is what I wish." said Amani.

The room fell silent. Such a magnitude of a question must take some time to answer. She imagined him pacing the room, choosing his words carefully, thinking of his long, thoughtful explanation. She imagined maps and drawings, long parchments filled with the grand design of the world and her place in it. Even if it is small, it will bring her some comfort.

"...Jinn?...What say you?" said Amani.

The room was silent still. She turns around to confront him. "Jinn!" said Amani.

But the Jinn was gone.

"Jinn?... Jinn?!" screamed Amani.

She ran around the room, holding her torch high, looking everywhere for the Jinn. But she could find nothing. The Jinn had vanished, leaving her with an empty hole in her heart.

Leaving her unanswered in this unknowable universe. Exhausted and defeated, Amani lay on the ground. She placed her torch beside her, staring deep into the flame as if the answer were there. Slowly, the fire began to die out, and she was engulfed in darkness. She never moved, and she never cried. She just lay there until her final moments.

The House of Crow

In the town of Junee
Walk up the stone steps
To the House Of Crow
And enter the home

Notice the red carpet
With its maroon patterns
How it clashes with the wallpaper
Yellow like decaying flesh

Late Victorian
And standing upon the hill
Looking above the town
 A lovely family

Ellen greets you
Giving you a cold glance over
Respect her home
She rules with an iron fist

Go up the stairs to Charles's room
Head of the family
Loved by everyone
 Forever unfaithful

The maid is there
Standing in the corner
She is pregnant
It was not her choice

Head to the balcony
Coming from the stables
The sound of chains
A boy chained to the wall

He thrashes about
Screaming in pain
Forever malformed
From terrible luck

The smell of flames
Over to the coach house
Where a fire blazes
And the smoke rises

Out of the coach house
Comes a man named Malcolm
Covered in flames
Scorch marks in the grass

Go back down the hall
 Baby Edith on the stairs
 Go to grab her
But she tumbles all the same

Look down the stairs
And she is gone
All that remains
Are stains on the floor

A gunshot rings
 Go out to the porch
And find the body
Of poor old Jack

The players gathers
For poor old Jack
For he is the newest
 To join the family

They welcome him in
He stands and joins them
One of the family
For all oblivion

Walk down the stone steps
 Walk up the road
Never return
To House of Crow

Family

I am reading *Moby Dick* in my study. It is night, and the moon shines so brightly through the windows. It feels as though God himself is casting his lonesome eye upon me. Checking on me to see if I am doing well, the last son of the Kudela family line. The fireplace is roaring, and a nice tint of orange shades the room. The house creaks like the bones of an old man, taking one last stretch before the passing of a new day.

After my parents' death and my brother moved away from our tiny town, I inherited the family home. I have lived in this home all my life: I was raised here and plan to die here. I am 70 years old and all I have wanted is to be alone. My parents had lofty positions in their time. My father was a surgeon and philanthropist, and my mother was his right-hand man. She would host charity balls and organize rallies to protest the issues of the day.

My brother followed suit in these exploits, traveling to Africa to help build homes for those in need. In fact, the Kudela family legacy is filled with tales of grandeur, those who trod their own path, beat their own drum and built their fortunes from the ground up. My grandmother worked on the Manhattan Project, and my grandfather was a war hero during WWII. My great-grandfather was an oil tycoon, and my great-great-grandparents helped slaves in the Underground Railroad. Before that, generations of Kudelas were great warriors and kings back in their home country. Of Slavic descent, the Kudela's are a legendary family.

"*And what have I done?*" you ask. Surely, with such an illustrious family heritage, I, too, would aspire to greatness. But alas, I do not. I have never wanted their lives, for I despise my family. They are a bunch of murderers and thieves whose ego governs their every move. Afraid to live in the shadows lest they miss out on the spotlight. All eyes must always be upon them, and they became angry children if they did not get what they wanted—stomping about, throwing fits. I have seen my fair share in my lifetime from my parents, brother, and relatives. I was always the black sheep, the butt of the joke. I had no aspirations of greatness and wanted a quiet, simple life. And now that my family is gone, the ridicule is over. Their voices no longer rumble in my head. My father, telling me that I am not worthy of the family name. My mother's

passive-aggressive tone echoing a bit too loud when talking about me to her friends in the parlor. And my brother, his bullying words were thrown at me like baseballs.

No more. No more do they rule my life. I have this home; its empty halls do not taunt me.

I have removed the family photos and stored away the family heirlooms. It is my own space. I will watch as the wood rots and the cobwebs form and take great pleasure from it. The only untouched area is the vast collection of books in the large study room. From floor to ceiling, each shelf is covered with thousands of books, encircling me in a wealth of knowledge and escapism—books all around, collected throughout the ages. I cannot wait to spend my final days reading these beautiful books. In addition to the family home, I have also inherited the family fortune. There is no need to work, no need to survive, no need to suffer. There is simply time to live, to enjoy.

Sitting in my reading chair, I take a sip of tea from the side table and look over to the window curtains. I notice a slight movement, a rustle of the linen. I do not have any animals in the house, so it startles me quite a bit. Then, out from the shadows, he steps into the moonlight. The Domovoy. A house spirit that resides over a home and protects the family within. But what makes him so special is that he *is* family. The first family member of the Kudela family, from the dawn of time itself. Sent from the netherworld to watch over us, give good fortune, and ensure we prosper. I suppose the jig is up: this is the secret to my family's success. I did not believe it, mind you. And my family made sure to scold me about my disbelief. How I did not keep my moment of silence before dinner to honor the Domovoy, or that I did not provide my proper offerings of milk and honey before bed. I was a boy of knowledge, of science. They were a people of the old faiths.

The Domovoy is small, the size of a small child, with long stringy hair and a big bushy beard. He is old, with wrinkly skin and calloused fingers and toes. He is naked, always crouching, constantly crawling. He comes towards me on his hands and knees. As he does so, the fire dies out, and darkness envelops the room. He does not look pleased. I am frozen with fear.

The wheels of time have stopped as I wait for my decrepit ancestor to lay his judgment on me. He crouches at the feet of the chair, stares up into my eyes, and speaks.

"Where are you?" asks the Domovoy. "...I beg your pardon?" I ask.

"Where are you?" he asks again, irritated. "Oh, uh, in my private library?" I reply.

"No! Where are you in the family tree?!" he yells.

"Ah! I see! I am the last in the line of the Kudela family." I reply, scared for my safety. "Where are the other members?" he asks.

"They have passed, I'm afraid." I reply.

"Tragic. What of your wife? Children?" he asks.

"None to speak of. I live alone here. It is a quiet life, but it is mine," I reply.

"Nonsense. I am the keeper of the line and the protector of this family. My name is long forgotten, even to myself. If you wish to keep my employment, to instill good fortune and prosperity, you must continue the line." he said, almost puffing his feeble chest out in pride.

"Well… then consider your employment…fulfilled? The family is long gone, and the need for protection is no longer necessary." I said.

Silence fills the room. Staring up at me with those primordial eyes like I was some abnormality he could not place his finger on.

"What do you do?" he asked me, clearly irritated. "…I am retired." I replied.

"What *did* you do?" he pushed.

"I was an accountant. I helped my father part-time with his investments, but I mainly worked with private clients and their finances." I replied.

"Is that how it is you wish to be remembered? Numbers and the like?" he asked. "I do not need to be remembered. I am perfectly content with living a comfortable existence." I replied.

"That is not what the Kudela family was built on." he said. "And what was it built on?" I asked.

"Blood, conquest, and retribution. The foundation of all things. These you must do if you want to continue the line." he said.

I could hear my family in his voice. My father, mother, brother, and the entire Kudela family rested in his voice on his tongue. He truly is family, and that makes me furious.

"Have you ever read this novel here?" I asked.

I held up my copy of *Moby Dick* and handed it down to him to look at.

"I don't do much reading." he said.

"Moby Dick, Frankenstein, and The Great Gatsby, these novels tell the stories of men and their ambitious exploits. Only for reality to set in and their ambitious nature to be their downfall. How they pushed away the ones they loved, friends, and relations alike. Some of them even die throughout the story. Finally, when reaching the climax, it all crumbles upon them, resulting in their failure. Or, in these instances, their deaths."

The ire is rising in my voice, unbidden.

"And for what? To have their names inscribed upon the pages of history? No, sir, not for me. The world is tragic enough as it is. I do not feel the need to add to that tragedy out of some necessity to fulfill my ego or to whatever society believes *I* owe. I owe nothing to them, to the family, and certainly not to *you*. But as much as I hate to admit it, you are still family. And I will not kick you out of your home. As long as you keep your distance,

I think we will get along just fine." the anger still in my voice.

The Domovoy looks at me with the uttermost intensity. I swear, his eyes could cut through me like Excalibur. Then, he starts to laugh. A mixture of gravel and honey reverberates throughout the room. Without taking his eyes off of me, slowly, he retreats his way back to the window, back into the shadows. He doesn't say a word and sulks back into his corner until he vanishes. The laughing stops, the fire lights ablaze, and I am left alone with the sound of crackling wood and the creaking of an old house.

***

Over the next few months, I catch him in the corner of my vision. Hiding behind the curtains, in the closet, peeking around a corner, or underneath the stairs. Always with those hateful eyes. Sometimes, I swear, I hear him mumble something—some snide comment.

"Worthless." "Lazy." "Disgrace."

It's like living with my family again. Every movement I make, cooking, cleaning, walking, breathing, any moment of rest, is regarded as an act of treason upon the family name. I hate him, but God knows I dare not kill him. He may not protect me anymore, but killing a Domovoy would bring me pain and suffering. I could never live in peace ever again.

And so, the Domovoy stays. The only comfort I can gather is that he, too, will follow suit in the moment of my inevitable demise. Once the family line is destroyed, the Domovoy has fulfilled his purpose. Until then, the old curmudgeon must tolerate my existence as I have come to tolerate his.

***

I am on the cusp of falling asleep in my bed and suddenly feel a heaviness in my chest. I try to take a breath, and I simply can not. I open my eyes and see him there, crouching upon my chest, smoking a cigar, and staring off into space. *I'm dreaming.*" I think to myself. I am no stranger to nightmares, and I have read all about sleep paralysis and the awful things that people hallucinate. But no, I am pretty sure he is real.

"I had to lead my first raiding party when I was a young man. We were not even men yet, in the literal sense. Neanderthals, fighting aimlessly in this shit-storm of a world. They were the ones that started it—attacking our settlement at night, taking our food, taking our women, killing our children. I believe that those moments were the beginning of humanity because we did not simply rebut with an attack. Oh no. We had "ambition" as you like to put it. "Creativity" about what we were going to do them. First, we took over the encampment. Then, we tied up the men and tortured them. Then, we killed all the women right in front of them. Some were even ours, but we made them watch all the same. Then, we took their young and threw them into a large fire we had built. We made them watch that, too. Made them listen to the screams of their dying young. Then we cut off their manhoods and threw them into the fire. Then we left them there. I left them for their gods to bear witness and silently judge as we took back what was ours—all my idea. I became the leader of that tribe, and that is how the Kudela family was born. *That* is your legacy. That is what this family was built on. Conquest, revenge, and pride. Take what is yours because no one will hand it to you. And you choose to sit there, in your books. Well…we'll have to change that." said the Domovoy, taking a drag of his cigar.

I blink, and he vanishes. The air returned to my lungs, and I held my chest tight in pain.

***

Several more months have passed since that incident. And since then, I have come to see him less and less. Every now and again, I will see him peeking around the corners, staring at me. But no more under the stairs, behind the curtains, or in the closet. Perhaps being persistent in my ways, he lost interest. Maybe he will fade away on his own, and the memory of the Kudela family will be forgotten to the sands of time. I even found him in the library once. I was about to enter the room when I noticed him sitting in my chair. I peeked around the corner, and to my surprise, he was reading. *Moby Dick,* to be exact. A glimmer of hope washed over me. Maybe there is a chance for him to change his ways. Perhaps he considered what I had to say the other night about ambition and decided to read the books I had mentioned. Maybe he regretted what he had told me the other night and is trying to make up for past sins. I left him alone with the hope that things might turn for the better.

***

I wake up to the sun shining in my eyes. God's watchful eye casts upon me once again and with fiery intensity. I lift myself, get ready for the day, and maybe pay a visit to the "old man," as I have come to call him now. But as I lift myself, I realize that, yet again, there is another heaviness on my chest. I look up to find a stack of books. I lift them and put them on my nightstand. The Domovoy has left them here for me. "*Maybe he read these and wanted me to read them?*" is my first thought. I get out of bed to go and find the "old man," only to find myself stepping on another book. And as I look out in the hallway, I see a trail of books leading down the stairs. I follow it, one book after the other. All of these books lead me to their resting place. I enter the library, afraid of what I have found. Piles and piles of books. All of them are removed from the shelves and neatly stacked— thousands and thousands of words, a maze of literature, ceiling high. And I know he is in here.

"You know something? I have quite enjoyed this reading thing. You learn a lot." said the Domovoy.

I spin around and try to find where his voice is coming from. The books encircle me like buildings in a massive city. I wade through the towers of paper, searching for my ancient relative.

"And, what it is exactly that you have learned?" I asked.

I need to keep him talking, to find him. I have put up with my "house guest" for long enough, and now I believe it is about time he left. I do not care if bad luck befalls me for the rest of my life—better bad luck than no luck at all.

"I read the books you told me about the first night we met: *Frankenstein*, *Moby Dick*, and *The Great Gatsby*. I read as these men strived to achieve greatness, only to lead to their inevitable downfall. And I thought, "Maybe the lad was right?" So I started to read more, and I noticed something. A pattern. Each character received a glorious death, and their names were written down in history. Then it dawned on me…death is the only way to preserve your legacy. Death is the reassurance that we were here and that we did something. And with a glorious death comes remembrance. You have lived a life of shelter and safety. But there is still time for you, and there is still time for a glorious death. I cannot watch you waste your life away any longer.

Watching you reading your books, cooking your breakfast, sitting alone, with complete disregard for your life, makes me sick. So what will it be? Shall I chop you into pieces with the axe out by the woodshed? Should I split your jaw open with my bare hands? Maybe I'll hang you like a pig on a hook and watch as your body drains off your blood? Or maybe I'll tie you to a post and cut off your manhood? Like I did to those Neanderthals when I was a young man. Death is your only salvation." said the Domovoy.

I cannot find him, and I cannot see him. I can hear his voice echoing throughout the room. He could be hiding behind the books, he could be behind the curtains, in the walls, or under the floorboards.

"You forget! If I die, you die with me! I am the last of the line, and you'll fade away!" I scream.

"Will I? I imagine it'll become quite a story when they find your mangled body here. The man who was brutally murdered in his own home under mysterious circumstances. This house will become a legend, and everyone will want to come to this neighborhood to see the famed Kudela house. That will be your legacy, and I will not be forgotten. Everyone will remember the Kudela name." crowed the Domovoy.

I hear shuffling, scuffles in the corner, every creak in the floor, and every gust of wind is a quick reaction. A jolt here, a flinch there. I'm looking behind every book, and I cannot find him. My doom is imminent. I can feel it. It's only a matter of time before he kills me in whatever nefarious way he has planned. My nerves are tingling, my eyes are hyperfocused, my head begins to pound, and I can feel the shortness of my breath. I can hear him laughing. It's growing louder and louder, more maniacal, more menacing. Getting closer and closer, but I cannot tell where he is. It's only a matter of time. After all, I will die like the men in those books. Ambitious in wanting to live my simple life, pushing away all of my loved ones, some of them even dying, until the ultimate climax. It's all crumbling around me, resulting in my failure. Or, in this case, my death.

The Seventh Son

I look up at the leafless trees, the branches extending outwards in jagged positions. It looks like lightning crackling in the sky. It is cold, and the autumn air stings my flesh. I have nothing but a shirt on and my trousers. But there are other ways a man can stay warm. The bottle of rum in my hand has given me plenty of warmth, more than some overcoat. I am alone, and that is how I want it to be. I walk up the path, looking at the autumn leaves on the ground. The reds, yellows, and oranges are so beautiful. I put the bottle to my lips and take a mighty swig of rum. I am becoming dizzy and losing my balance. The sweet embrace of death awaits, and I look forward to never seeing this godforsaken place again. But as I walk, I begin to hear a strange noise. A noise that one would not think to hear in the forest. The sound of chains. Chains dragged along in the dirt, banging against the rocks and twigs. And that's when I notice the hushed silence across the land. The insects are quiet, and the breeze has all but vanished. Then the clouds start moving over the moon till darkness envelopes the land. What was once a beacon for weary travelers now hides behind the smoke of God. I pick up my pace and try to get to the river as quickly as possible. But as I walk faster, I hear another sound: laughter. It starts small, like a whisper. Gradually picking up in intensity until it completely takes over the silence. A deep, menacing laugh, full of malice and malcontent. Now I begin to run and drop my bottle to the ground. Over every stone and every branch, my feet crunch over autumn leaves, and I run like the devil at my back. Because, for all I know, he is.

I trip on a branch, and I fall to solid earth. I lie there, waiting for my tormentor to send me to whatever hell awaits. The laughing, the clanging of chains, they come closer and closer. I am frozen, I am afraid to look up, and I am ready to die.

"Get up." said the most angelic voice.

I look up, and I see her. The Cadejo, the black dog. She is massive, the size of a cow.

With shaggy black hair, long sharp teeth, her huge tongue hung down, and she had goat hooves instead of paws. And the stench, worse than any smell you can imagine. I stand up as quickly as possible, staring at my tormentor with whatever courage I have left. I do not even come close to her height. Even standing, she towers over me by several feet.

"I do not know what you plan to do, but do it quick!" I scream.

"I mean you no harm, human. You are in danger, and we need to be off." she said urgently.

"Are you going to kill me?" I ask.

"No, but *he* will if we do not move." she says.

She turns around and begins to walk down the path, expecting me to follow behind. "And if I choose not to move?" I press.

"You are welcome to stay there and find out for yourself." she says, anger in her voice.

I am ready to die, but perhaps not in the manner she is implying. Whatever is following me may intend to harm not just my person, but my soul. So I grab my rum and catch up to the Black Cadejo.

***

We walk for about an hour in silence, the sound of rustling leaves and chains filling the air every few minutes. I can hear that laughter behind me. I hear it whispered in my ear, but there's nothing there every time I turn around.

"I know where you walk. I know you seek to end your life at the river's edge." says the black dog.

"How do you know?" I ask.

"Everywhere the White Cadejo goes, death follows it. Its stench lingers in the air when he is around. You also carry the scent of death, the death of lovers. Why must your life end, my child?" she asked.

"My family has all but left me, and they abandoned me on our church's doorstep when I was born. I was born the seventh son of the seventh son. Bad luck, bad for any family. They moved away shortly after. I was raised in the church and kept in the cellar. Fed the scraps and waste of the others, I might as well have been born an animal. As much as people like to protect children, for whatever reason, orphans are a different story. Especially when you are the seventh son, a bad omen. Oh, they tried to blame me. A cow was killed, a child went missing, or any bad luck out of human control, "It was that damn kid," they said. I would tell them I did nothing, but they would claim I was lying. And they would beat and starve me, hoping I would die one day.

But I would not. I still do not know why they just did not kill me. I think they are cowards—all of them. Instead of putting a creature out of misery, God wants us to preserve life at all costs. I had to suffer so that they could maintain their beliefs.

When I was 17, I escaped. The priest did not latch the door properly, and it was a Tuesday afternoon, so the church was empty, and the priest was in the village performing the last rites of a prisoner. I escaped, leaving that village forever and entering the city. Begging for food and sleeping in the streets, I soon became addicted to the drink. Wherever I could get it, sometimes trading my food for that sweet nectar, this world had done nothing but beat me down with no forgiveness. The old gods have abandoned me. God has left me. Tonight I finally found the courage, and I shall end it all. This trail leads to a river, and I shall drink this bottle of rum till I can no longer stand and throw myself into the river. I will drown a tortured, worthless man with nothing to show for his life. A life that I was thrust into with no choice of my own. In my own way, I became the very thing they always said I was: a monster." I explain.

"Do you see me as such a creature? Do you look upon the Cadejos as a monster?" she asks.

"Well…might I ask, where are your chains and glowing red eyes? And, why have you not torn me limb from limb? I have heard that Cadejos like to play with their prey, but never this much." I pressed.

"You are mistaking me for *him*. I am the Cadejo of the right-handed path, the follower of light. While the other Cadejo is of the left-handed path, the follower of darkness." she explained.

"But I do not understand. How come your fur is black if you are on the side of good?" I asked.

"Things are not always as they seem. Just like you, little one. You have been cursed for a life of evil, yet you are a good man. Troubled, broken, but good nonetheless. But the world lives in the grey." she said.

"What do you mean?" I ask.

"Would there be no good without bad? Would there be no joy without pain? Would there be no sweet without sour? Evil must always exist. It takes on the burden that so few are willing to carry. Your village may have been cast out, but now they have faith. They can move about the world with goodness in their heart and be certain they vanquished evil for the afternoon. It is the oldest story ever told. Good versus evil. Every tribe, village, city, and person feels they are the good, and the other is the bad. All the while, they were unaware that they might be bad for someone else. Never underestimate the lines between good and evil and all that lies in the middle." she explained.

Just as she finishes explaining, the laughter begins again. This time, only louder. The jangling of chains fills the air. The two together are an orchestra of madness.

"Filling his head with nonsense, I see." said a voice from the trees.

We stop dead in our tracks. That voice is like knives to my nerves. We look all around us, trying to find the white dog. Trees rustle, bushes shake, a laugh, a rattle of chains. They seem to come from everywhere all at once.

"There is no escape. I will have you. You and your alcoholic friend. Tonight will be the last time you and I ever have to face each other." said the white dog.

He steps out of the foliage and onto the road. He is the same in appearance and size as the black dog, except, of course, for his white fur. Even though white symbolizes purity and good, I feel much fear and evil from this creature. The white overtakes the darkness, confident in its appearance. It has no fear of predators because it is the predator. It has no fear of being seen because it wants to be seen. He snarls at me, growls, and shows his even whiter teeth, sharpened to the edge and ready to tear through flesh. No concern for my past or my future. Just the next meal, the next soul.

"The battle between good and evil will end once and for all," he says.

Then he lunges for me. I am helpless, frozen with fear. Only the black dog dares to take action and step in front of me. The two wrestle, writhing around on the ground. I remember once when I was a boy, down in that basement, I found a book. It was called the *Toa Te Ching*. And in it, there was a symbol. Black and white encircling each other but never joining in formation. A representation of yin and yang, the good and bad. Always separate but dependent on each other. All I could see in their struggle was the yin and the yang—teeth sunken into one another, blood splattering, staining the other's fur. The sound of guttural growls and barks fills the air, sending shivers down my spine. I run as fast as I can down the dark path. After what I have witnessed, I cannot live this life anymore. I am cursed, doomed to live this life in exile and misery. I cannot do it. I will take the only thing I control and drown it in the river. It is just up ahead. I can see it now. I can hear the river running and smell the fresh water. Soon, it will be all over.

I hear the sound of a whimper and then dead silence. No more fighting, no more snarling, just silence. In my heart, I know one of them is dead. I turn around toward the path and await the victors' arrival. The wind began to blow through the trees, and the rustle of the leaves made me feel a calm that I had not felt all night. And then she arrives; the black dog. Covered in blood and injured. I go up to her.

"Are you alright?" I ask.

"I will be okay." she replies.

"The White Cadejo is dead?" I ask. "Yes." she replies.

"What now?" I ask.

"Balance must be restored. Without light, there cannot be darkness. And without the dark, the light cannot shine. Someone must be the White Cadejo, and that someone is you." she said.

"No! I am done with this life! I am going to that river and ending myself and my worthless existence!" I scream.

"It does not have to be worthless. You know what it is to walk down a lonely path, an angry path, a path filled with regrets and unresolved issues. You know what it means to be persecuted and to be feared. People need something to fear, something to hate. They need evil to feel the potential for good." she explained.

She gets up and runs off into the forest. Suddenly, the moon emerges from the clouds, slicing the darkness away. It casts its light upon me, and I begin to transform. I drop to the ground, and the pain is unbearable. I beg God for release, but he does not listen. It is like a fire running through my veins, and every bone in my body has been snapped. My neck begins to elongate, my arms and legs extend, my ears grow into pig ears, my hands into hooves, my skin boils as I grow white fur, and my eyes bleed as they turn blood red. I look like a cross between a wild pig and a feral dog. Ears and snout of a pig, hooves of a pig, but the body of a wolf, with razor-sharp teeth and blood-red eyes.

The pain ceases, and I am now what I swore never to become. The internal struggle of light versus dark continues, the world turns, and the substance of the universe continues to ebb and flow. I run off into the forest in my new beastly form.

Sweet Blood

"What do you mean she escaped?!" screamed my mother.

My mother, Rose, was an Italian immigrant from Sicily, who emigrated in 1940 at 20 years old to escape Mussolini. She was a seamstress with a storefront in downtown Boston that opened in 1945. The women came and went with their weddings and important events. But no matter who walked in, she always treated them with the same bluntness. She didn't take shit from anybody. She had an attitude, and you did not mess around with my mother. You gave it to her straight and honest. Not like this clown doctor, who decided to tell my mother in the worst possible way that her mother, my grandmother, had escaped the mental asylum, we put her in.

"Well...l-like I said, Mrs. Junkosta...y-your mother...-" the doctor started to say.

"I heard ya! What I wanna know is how the hell this happened?! And how did it happen on your watch?!" screamed my mother.

"Rose, relax!" screamed my father.

My father, Zoel, also had enough of Mussolini and left Italy in 1941 at 21. His real last name is Jocasta, but the immigration officers at Ellis Island couldn't understand my father with his thick accent and misheard it as "Junkosta," So that's what they wrote on the immigration form. My father was a stoic man, never gave anyone trouble, and always had a calming charm. He didn't question the guard and used the name to his advantage. He opened a mechanic shop in 1947, and he called it Hunk O' Junk. The customers fell in love with him, always fixing their troubles and washing their worries away. That's where he fell in love with my mother after she almost beat one of his employees with a tire iron after "overcharging her for her oil change." At least, that's what she claims. They married in 1948, and in 1951 I was born. But I wasn't the first. They tried once before, but it ended in miscarriage. I was their miracle child. Ten years later, here we are, my father, having to stop my mother from beating another man to death.

"Don't you tell me to relax! This is my mother! Now where is she?!" she screamed. "I am trying to tell you to Mrs. Junkosta, and we don't know where she is! We're not even sure how she got out! Twenty-four-seven security, the latest security systems, guards at the front door, the receptionist, no one saw her leave, and the cameras have nothing. And the police have already searched the grounds! She seems to have vanished into thin air." said the doctor.

"Maybe it was the fairies?" I said quietly.

"Matty! Don't start with that nonsense again, or we'll put you in here too!" yelled my mother.

My mother had to leave alone, and they didn't have the money to all travel together. So her mother and father came later, Lillian and Joseph. They lived as pig farmers in the countryside and grew tomatoes. Soon Mussolini and his army took over. His soldiers would visit their little cottage once a month and raided their house to ensure they weren't spies for the enemy. And they made sure to help themselves to the garden or whatever else they wanted. Whatever goods they had left, they would take to the market to sell. Eventually, in 1957, when I turned 6, they raised enough money and were able to move to the States with my folks. I got close to my grandparents. My grandfather gave me lots of candy and told me he used to be an enforcer for the mafia. But then he met my grandmother and left that life behind him. My parents used to tell me that wasn't true, but I think they didn't want me to believe he was a bad guy.

But it's my grandmother who I was really close with. My grandma used to tell me stories, and one of those stories, was of the Doñas de fuera, the Ladies from the Outside. The fairies. She told me that the fairies came out of their homes when the war began. They lived inside the rolling hills, and when the bombs dropped, their homes were destroyed. The fairies started to take residence in people's homes, in secret, mind you. Very rarely did they reveal themselves, only to certain people. People she called "sweet bloods." If you had sweet blood, it meant you had a little bit of fairy inside of you. Very rarely did men have sweet blood. It was mostly women who had it. And boy, did my grandmother have it. She said the fairies revealed themselves to her constantly. They were the most glorious creatures she ever saw, with features of someone young in their prime. They would pick vegetables together and walk through the hills. They even showed her where their old home used to be. In a hill right behind her home. They were dressed in white, and they had the paws of cats. They always came in a group of seven; sometimes, one would play the lute for her. She said it was the most beautiful sound in the world and always brought a tear to her eye every time she heard it. My grandfather never saw them and never heard them. But he never questioned his wife. He knew better than to deny the old tales, the old religions. They even saved her life.

My grandfather was selling goods in the city, and my grandmother was at home doing the laundry. During one of the Nazi raids, they dragged my grandmother out of the house and brought her to the barn. The Nazis were craving milk, and they wanted my grandmother to milk one of the cows so they could have fresh milk. But when they brought her out there, she was too nervous. She could barely move, let alone speak. They became irritated with her and eventually beat her in that barn. They beat her with sticks and whips, bleeding out on the ground, whimpering in pain. And after that, they left. They didn't even care about the milk anymore. She crawled out of the barn and back to the house, a trail of blood dragging behind her. She passed out at the front door from the pain, and my grandfather came home several hours later. They had no money for medicines or treatments. All he could do was watch her suffer and help her rest. But the fairies, they knew what to do. With their ancient magic, they nursed her back to health.

When they raised enough money, selling off their pigs to neighbors and selling vegetables at the market, they were sad to say goodbye. They left the house to the fairies and didn't want to sell it off to somebody else for fear of the fairies being homeless. They left them some bread and wine as a sign of respect and left for America. They never found out what happened to the house.

My mother and father always wave these stories off as old superstitions. But my grandmother believed it, and that was good enough for me. 2 years after they moved here, my grandfather passed away. Heart attack, really tragic. The loss hurt everyone, but my grandmother was devastated. Not long after, she started having these dreams. The dream always started the same, and she was flying through the air with a group of women riding on goats. They would fly together through the clouds, over the ocean, until finally, they reached an island. They would land there and be greeted by a red-colored teenage boy and a beautiful woman who sat on a throne.

"Hello, Lillian, welcome to our kingdom. I am the King, and this is my Queen." said the red-colored teenage boy.

"Where am I?" asked my grandmother.

"You are in the Kingdom of Naples, or as we call it, Benevento. We want to propose an offer." said the beautiful woman.

Then one of the women riding the goats approached my grandmother and offered her a cup of wine.

"This is Ensign, the leader of the Doñas de fuera. She was like you once, a human, a "sweet blood," as you have come to call it. We saw that she was pure of heart and offered her a choice. Drink from the chalice, drink the wine from Benevento's fruits, and become a fairy. And now we offer this choice to you." said the Queen.

"I do not understand." said my grandmother.

"You are pure of heart, Lillian. The Doñas de fuera, who you so graciously accepted into your home and took care of, spoke of you in such high regard. They love you as much as you love them, and we would be honored to add you to our ranks. As one of the only males to receive this gift, I do not need to stress how rare of an honor this is. But please, take your time to think. We will be waiting." said the King.

Then the dream ends. Every day she would talk about the fairies to us and anyone she could tell. She would talk about Benevento, she would speak of the King and the Queen, and after a while, it took a toll on my parents. People were asking questions, regular clients didn't want to go to my mom and dad anymore, and a reputation was beginning to spread. That my grandmother was a witch, consorting with the devil.

They sent her off to a mental asylum a year after the dreams started, hoping they could find a cure for her. The doctors had all kinds of theories: repressed grief from the death of her husband, or even that the dreams represented her wanting to return to Italy, Benevento being her home, and the King and the Queen being the manifestation of her nostalgia. Bunch of bullshit if you ask me. I believe my grandmother, and she didn't need a bunch of doctors telling her otherwise. And wouldn't you know it, the dreams never stopped. We would visit her occasionally, and she would talk about the fairies. But I remember one visit in 1959, and she told us that the dream had changed. She said she felt like she had more control over her dream.

Whereas before, it felt more like a vision the fairies were showing her. The dream went as normal. Looking into the eyes of the King and Queen, she could smell the fresh air and feel the chalice of wine in her hands. But before the dream ended, that crazy lady did it. She drank from the cup. She became a fairy. Once the doctors heard of this, they knew the dreams would end soon. They claimed that the drink represented her acceptance of reality and that it was time to move on. I swear, I think they just make this stuff up. But even still, the dreams didn't stop. She started to become restless, screaming all through the night, and slamming on the walls. During lunch, she would throw her food; during her leisure hour, she would hit the orderlies until she had to be dragged back to her room. We were certain she went off the deep end. Ever since then, we have visited her less and less. It became too painful, and we wanted to remember her as she was, not how she became. A whole year went by with not so much as a peep from the hospital. We paid our bills to the asylum, and they kept her locked up. It kept me awake at night, thinking about her alone, with only her dreams to keep her company. I wanted to convince my parents to lets us see her. But then we got the call from the asylum that it concerned my grandmother and that we needed to arrive as quickly as possible.

***

"So what are we supposed to do now?!" screamed my mother.

"Well, the police have put out an APB for your mother, and they have police cars searching the area for her as we speak." explained the doctor.

"She's not a criminal Doctor, and she needs help! She's sick!" yelled my mother.

"Yes, we are well aware, Mrs. Junkosta. Just a few days ago, she bit one of the orderlies, causing serious injury. Because of that, we had to give her shock therapy to calm her nerves." explained the doctor.

That did not sit well with my mother. She stared at him in awe, like some creature from another world. She couldn't believe what she was hearing. My father knew that look; it was the same before she beat Vincenzo with the tire iron.

"Is that what you do here? Someone's a little too resistant, and you give them a shock? I don't know if I believe my mother, but I would rather hear her crazy stories than watch her rot in here. Electric shock therapy?! She's an old woman talking about fairies?! You people don't know what you're doing. When we find her, we're taking her back." explained my mother.

"Really mom?! Grandma is coming back with us?!" I said. She kneeled close to me, looking me deep in the eyes. "You bet, honey." she said with a smile.

I gave her a big hug. I couldn't believe it! I let her go and hugged my dad as well. He had a smile on his face too. We were going to be a family again.

"Doctor! Doctor!" screamed a voice from the hall. Running into the room was a police officer, drenched in sweat.

"Please, all of you, come with us right away! We found her! It was the last place we would have thought!" screamed the officer.

"Where?!" screamed my mother. "The roof!" replied the officer.

We all ran out together. My mother held my hand, dragging me across the hall as we got to the stairs that led to the roof. My father, the doctor, and the officer were not far behind us. Up we went, 4 flights of stairs, and there she was. Standing on the roof's edge looking down on the rose garden the other patients planted. The fall would seriously injure her even if it didn't kill her. Some other cops were standing right below her.

"Ma'am, please! Turn around, go down the stairs, and find the nearest doctor! Let us help you!" screamed a cop with a megaphone.

"You can't help me! I need to see my daughter!" screamed my grandmother. "Mom!" my mother screamed.

Grandma turned around to face us, and she had a huge smile on her face. "Hi, honey! I finally got out!" my grandma screamed.

"I can see that!" Now can you please come to us so we can take you home!" yelled my mother.

"But I *am* going home! I'm going to live with the fairies! They're on their way right now, coming to get me and take me to Benevento! I'll be home soon enough!" yelled my grandmother.

The cop stood behind my mother, handcuffs at the ready. And the doctor stood beside him with a syringe filled with God knows what.

"Grandma, please! We're gonna take you home! You're gonna live with us now! No more hospitals! Please!" I screamed.

She looked at me, and her smile faded. A tear began to fall from her eye. And then she jumped.

She jumped off that roof, plummeting to the rose bush below. I imagined her corpse bouncing on the ground, scrapes and bruises riddling her body. I began to cry as her body disappeared from my sight. My mother screamed, and we all ran to the roof's edge. I was expecting the officers to be checking her body for any sign of life.

"Maybe she'd be okay?" I thought.

But there's no way they would let us take her back. They'll lock her up, and I'll never see her again.

But when we got to the edge, we looked down, and she wasn't there. The cops on the ground were dumbfounded, and they had watched her fall and then disappear.

"Where is she?!" screamed my mother.

"She just...vanished... mid-air!" the officer from below screamed. "Bullshit! She has to be there!" screamed my father.

"Look!" I screamed.

I looked up at the setting sun to find my grandmother floating in the air. The orange-red sun illuminated her. She looked like an angel. Slowly, she made our way down to us. She was so graceful, lowering herself back onto the roof. The doctor and the officer were dumbfounded, jaw to the floor. My mother's eyes were wide with disbelief. My grandmother walked up to my mother and hugged her.

"Mom…how is this possible?" asked my mother.

"You didn't believe me. But you've always been hard-headed. You've always been strong. Never let them take you down. Please don't make my mistake. Promise me." said my grandmother.

My mother squeezed her tight, tears streaming down her face. I have not seen my mom cry before or since. Then she walked up to my father.

"You take care of my daughter, you hear?" she said.

He gave her a big hug, a smile draped across his face. Then she walked up to me and kneeled to my level. I had tears running down my face. Deep in my heart, I knew this was the last time I would ever see her.

"Oh, Matty, don't cry." she said.

"I don't want you to go, Grandma." I said.

"Don't worry, Matty. I will always be there for you." she said. She kissed me on the forehead and then stood up.

"I love you all very much. Goodbye for now." she said.

She lifted her arms to the sky and slowly lifted off the ground. She floated up to the sun, glowing brighter than any star in the night sky. All of a sudden, women riding on goats appeared from thin air. They were gorgeous, and they were all giggling. They approached my grandmother, and before our eyes, she transformed from an old woman into a woman of 20. She got on top of one of the goats and waved goodbye to us. We watched her as she rode off into the sunset, making her way to Benevento.

***

That night, I had a dream. I was flying through the air on a goat and landed on a strange island. A red-colored teenage boy and a beautiful woman greeted me.

"Hello Matty, I am the Queen. We have heard so much about you." said the Queen. "I am the King. Please, won't you follow us." said the King.

And they led me through a field of sunflowers and lavender to a young woman sitting in the middle. It was my grandmother, and I was in Benevento.

"Grandma!" I screamed.

She turned around, and she had the biggest smile when she saw me. I ran toward her and crashed into her arms. I held her tight, never wanting to let her go. I looked up at her, crying tears of joy. And she only had one thing to say.

"I told you, Matty, I will always be with you."

Epilogue

The light began to fade, and the web vanished into the darkness.

"Okay, my boy, I believe you have enough stories to quench yourself of boredom for a lifetime. I believe it is time you return to your village." said Anansi.

"It has been an honor, great Anansi, and I will tell everyone in my village of all the wonderful stories you have told me. And I will tell them of your generosity." said Kweku.

"They may not believe your tale, but most stories are not believed anyway." joked Anansi.

"It is funny that you would mention that Anansi. Do you mind if I ask you one last question before I go?" asked Kweku.

"Ask away." said Anansi.

"All of the stories, well, I was just curious, were they real? Did they really happen? Or were you just tricking me?" asked Kweku.

"Oh my boy, you are smarter than you look. Yes, I admit, I have tricked you. For what is a story but a trick? Stories are made to trick another person. But what makes stories so wonderful is that the person wants to be tricked. Tricked into believing that good conquers evil, that love will triumph, and that our lives have meaning. But some tricks are mean-spirited. Some tricks reveal the evil in all of us and the futility of life. Stories are lies, with the truth hidden inside. But maybe we must be tricked into a lie to find the truth. It is not enough to know the answers; we must also know why the answer is important. That is what stories are for. And whether or not the stories are real, I can tell you this, the truth is stronger than reality. It is the very foundation of which we stand upon. Without truth, no progress would be made, the gods would not exist, and you would not exist. Without truth, life would vanish. Go on, young man! Spread these stories across the land! Spread the truth!" shouted Anansi.

Kweku was teleported out of the hut and grown back to normal size. He then made his way back to his village, and he spread the good news to all who would listen.